Totally Bound Publishing books by Angela Addams

Wicked Distractions
Wicked Disclosure

I0571278

Wicked Distractions

WICKED DISCLOSURE

ANGELA ADDAMS

Wicked Disclosure
ISBN # 978-1-83943-883-7
©Copyright Angela Addams 2020
Cover Art by Louisa Maggio ©Copyright April 2020
Interior text design by Claire Siemaszkiewicz
Totally Bound Publishing

This is a work of fiction. All characters, places and events are from the author's imagination and should not be confused with fact. Any resemblance to persons, living or dead, events or places is purely coincidental.

All rights reserved. No part of this publication may be reproduced in any material form, whether by printing, photocopying, scanning or otherwise without the written permission of the publisher, Totally Bound Publishing.

Applications should be addressed in the first instance, in writing, to Totally Bound Publishing. Unauthorised or restricted acts in relation to this publication may result in civil proceedings and/or criminal prosecution.

The author and illustrator have asserted their respective rights under the Copyright Designs and Patents Acts 1988 (as amended) to be identified as the author of this book and illustrator of the artwork.

Published in 2020 by Totally Bound Publishing, United Kingdom.

No part of this book may be reproduced, scanned, or distributed in any printed or electronic form without permission. Please do not participate in or encourage piracy of copyrighted materials in violation of the authors' rights. Purchase only authorised copies.

Totally Bound Publishing is an imprint of Totally Entwined Group Limited.

If you purchased this book without a cover you should be aware that this book is stolen property. It was reported as "unsold and destroyed" to the publisher and neither the author nor the publisher has received any payment for this "stripped book".

WICKED
DISCLOSURE

Dedication

To Yendor, my heart and soul.

"The only way to get what you want from a man is through sex. Whether you use it as a bribe, as a threat or as a promise, it's the only real power a woman has. Anyone who tells you different is full of shit."

—Sabine Cowan, founder and CEO of Kitty Calls Escort Service

Chapter One

"Someone will see us," Trent breathed out the words, half a moan, as Sabine opened his pants.

"Yeah, maybe." She licked her lips, her hand on his cock making him jolt. "But no one will talk about it."

He opened his lips to mutter some other stupid shit then closed them again. Sabine licked him from balls to crown and he thought he was going to come from that alone. He tilted his head back, groaning when she sucked him, slowly gliding her lips over his shaft, swirling and flicking her tongue before easing his dick in. She pumped him, taking him past the gate of her throat, fucking him with her entire mouth. His brain misfired, thoughts fading to nothing but electric impulses of pleasure. She gently massaged his balls with her fingers, her moan vibrating along his cock. Everything coiled—his gut, his sac—ready to blow.

She slid his dick out of her mouth, slowly, pressing her tongue hard against his shaft, lingering to give him another couple of flicks just under the ridge of his crown. He sucked in a deep breath and looked down at her, her lips glistening and a wicked smile greeting him. His body uncoiled, pulling him back from the edge enough that he could think again. It would have been some embarrassing shit if he'd lost his load so quickly.

"I probably shouldn't be doing this. Conflict of interest," he said, then chastised himself. *Shut up, you stupid fucker. Shut up, shut up, shut up!* There was Sabine Cowan, CEO of an escort empire, heiress to a multi-corporation legacy and notoriously *hot* bad girl, on her knees with her lips…*oh fuck*…her lips wrapped around his… "*Fuck!*"

She popped her mouth off him again, the suction making him want to follow her, his dick bobbing, begging for more. "You're not working tonight," she said. She sat back on her heels and slid her hand up his chest, pushing him to sit down in his chair. "I wouldn't have invited you to my party if I thought you were on the clock."

"Why am I here, then?" His brain was exploding, lust driving his every thought. He watched her lips move, her tongue darting to lick the corner of her mouth.

"Well…"

She moved between his legs, pushing against his thighs, nipples popping like they'd explode out of her low-cut dress. He wished they would. He kept his hands gripped to the arms of his chair, not trusting himself to move and break the lusty spell she was weaving.

"You're here to see how I keep secrets, aren't you?"

"I'm here to get you to sign a confidentiality agreement." He nearly choked on those words. *Could that be any more of a buzz kill?* She'd refused to sign the agreement at their meeting earlier, scoffing at idle threats made on behalf of his boss.

She smiled, batting her lashes. "Well, I guess you're just going to have to convince me then, aren't you?" She took his balls into her palm, stroking one then the other. "You wanna fuck me, messenger boy?"

"Yeah," he croaked. *Screw the confidentiality agreement.*

She released him, pushing on his thighs to stand, her hand out to help him up. In a daze he took her offer, standing on wobbly legs, dick rock hard, leading the way.

"You might want to tuck that bad boy back in." Sabine chuckled. "We've gotta walk through a few crowds to get upstairs."

Confused, Trent glanced down, realizing in a daze what she was saying. He pushed his aching dick back into his pants and zipped up. He'd had blow jobs in his life. Many. But he'd never had one like that. It seemed as if Sabine had enjoyed it just as much as he had. Maybe he'd just gotten so used to his mundane sex life that he'd forgotten how good things could be. Either way, he wasn't going to put the brakes on this. He couldn't. This was a fantasy-in-the-making of epic proportions. And he believed Sabine when she said that discretion was a guarantee. Off the clock or not, he knew his boss would not be happy to hear that Trent had not only partied with the enemy but fucked her too.

And that potentially sobering thought—the risk of blowing everything he'd worked his ass off to achieve, a corner office as Morgan and Miller Limited's newest lead communications officer, a stellar and solid reputation for innovative promotional campaigns and the bank account to show for it—still wasn't enough to derail his lust.

The temptation was just too great.

Sabine had been a socialite first—a wealthy heiress who'd attracted the media spotlight for not only her stunning looks but also her outrageous behavior. Drugs, parties, sex tapes... She'd done it all. Done it and reveled in it. Her celebrity status alone made her a trophy bang, but add to that her smoking-hot body— voluptuous and plump in all the right places— combined with her I'm-gonna-fuck-your-brains-out aggression and Trent was a goner.

Sabine took him up the grand staircase, leading him, walking just a little ahead so he felt like her hand in his was more like a leash, guiding him in the right direction. Adam, her very watchful bodyguard, was standing a few steps up, flicking his gaze from Trent to Sabine, his frown firmly in place. Sabine paused long enough so she could lean in and say something quietly to the giant brute. Adam gave a tight nod, shifting to look straight ahead, like Trent didn't exist. With another sly smile over her shoulder at Trent, Sabine continued up. His dick was literally weeping for her.

There was another staircase leading to the next floor, probably where the master suite was, but Sabine didn't continue upward. Instead, she took him down the hall, wall sconces lighting their way. It was quieter up here, the sound of murmured voices from the many conversations muffled as they moved higher and deeper into the house.

The room she led him to was bigger than his hotel room, even bigger than his condo. But there was nothing suggesting a touch of Sabine, nothing that made him think she'd invited him into her own bedroom, her sanctuary. He didn't know why that bothered him. Why it would matter that she wanted to fuck in a generic room?

"Is this a client room?" He pushed away the feeling of jealousy that had reared, surprised that it was there at all. While downstairs had been all about socializing and harmless flirting, upstairs was a different story. If there was any doubt in his mind that her legitimate escort business was a cover for more nefarious shit, the multi-room traffic of girls and older men they'd passed on the second floor had been enough to tell him otherwise.

Sabine smiled when she faced him, her hand on the door to close it. "This is a guest room."

She shut out the rest of the party then moved toward him to run her hands up his body and wrap her arms around his shoulders, pressing her lips to his. He melted into her kiss. Finally, he could taste her. Any other thoughts dissolved when she slipped her tongue into his mouth, exploring, entangling. He moved his hands to her hips, then over her ass, lifting her so she could wrap her legs around his waist. Her skirt hiked up under his hands and he brushed flesh. *She isn't wearing any panties.*

"You're bare," he said as he pulled away from her mouth.

She cocked her head in a coy gesture, one he didn't believe for a second. "Yeah, I was hoping you'd figure that out sooner and slip your fingers in for a bit."

"Downstairs?" He was taken aback then chuckled at his own shock. "Finger you in front of everyone?"

Sabine wiggled her way out of his grasp, kicked off her shoes then climbed onto the bed, facing him on her knees. "You'd be surprised how few people notice those kinds of things. And the ones who do either enjoy the view or look away."

Trent yanked off his jacket and shoes then crawled onto the bed, invading her space, making her move so that she was holding herself up, leaning back on her hands, her legs partially spread.

"Well, it would be a good show if they did watch." What he was really thinking was, *I sure as shit hope no one recognized me.* Instead of blurting out his panicked thoughts, he distracted himself with Sabine, letting his dick do the thinking from that point on. He ran his hand up her calf then down her thigh, slipping the skirt of her dress back to her waist.

She laughed, dropping her head back, and opened her legs wider. He ignored her offer, bypassing the view of her pussy, those plump lips bare of hair with the glint of a piercing on her hood, in favor of her luscious fat tits. Finding her peaked nipples hard, he lowered his mouth, sucking her through her dress before nipping her between his teeth, taking her by surprise so that she whipped her head back up to meet his gaze. Something sparkled there—intrigue, curiosity. She watched him move from one breast to the other, latching on to the top of her dress, yanking it down so that her tits spilled out.

She moaned when he nipped again at the lush bud that was hard, impossibly hard. He flicked his tongue against it, sucking while he fondled her other breast with his hand, cupping as much as he could, her ample flesh spilling out of his palm. He alternated between the two, flicking and teasing. He could play with her nipples forever, sucking them until they were hot and rosy red, throbbing against his tongue.

"Eat me, messenger boy." She rocked her hips, nudging against him, making his cock pulse.

He pulled away with a smile, feeling cunning, triumphant. Sabine Cowan was as good as begging him to lick her clit. He obviously had to oblige. He spread her legs wider, holding her knees as he lifted them, pushing back until they were nearly touching the bed. Her pussy was gloriously splayed, wet, glistening, the piercing a diamond stud, hot as hell. He licked his lips and she moaned, the sound enough to make his cock throb. He lay down between her legs, flicking at the piercing, rolling it around with his tongue before moving to her clit to give her a good suck. He licked his way down, probing her hole, lapping her juice. He glanced up and caught her watching him as she played with her tits, teasing herself, her eyes hooded.

He slid his fingers deep inside, stroking her G-spot, giving her the right kind of pressure, servicing her with his tongue and his lips, so that her orgasm would rise just as his had. And right when he got her writhing, groaning, her breathing hard, her eyes closed and back arched, he stopped.

It took her a few seconds to realize what he'd done. She cracked open her eyes, watching him, snaking her hand down to finish the job he'd started.

"Nah uh, sweetie." He gave a shake of his finger while he unbuttoned his pants with his other hand. "You're going to come around my cock."

Sabine froze in place and gave him a slow, knowing smile. She wiggled herself out of her dress, tossing it over his shoulder to land in a heap on the floor. He pulled his pants off, then his boxers and socks, followed by his shirt. After giving him another once-over, she crawled to the other side of the bed, swaying her ass in a tantalizing manner. She opened a drawer on the bedside table and pulled something out. Turning to face him, she tossed it against his chest.

Condoms. A row of them.

Trent smiled, his cock jolting, eager to be sheathed. She crawled to him, slipping her mouth over his dick at the same time that she ripped a condom from the row. When she sucked her way off, he mourned the loss but knew something much better was coming. She slipped the condom on him then spun around, wiggling her ass. He didn't need more of an invitation. With hands on her hips, he thrust into her, his balls smacking her skin. He moaned as her pussy gripped him.

She lowered herself so her face was against the mattress, his thrusts rocking her, her tits swaying. She slipped her hand down her front, likely to rub her clit. He couldn't actually see her fingers, but the thought of her touching herself had his orgasm rising fast. He reached one hand around to play with one of her breasts, cupping it then gliding his thumb down to flick her nipple. She cried out, her pussy spasming hard and fast, her moans bringing him to climax and cum spewing into the condom. It was a great release after months of nothing but his hand.

He pulled out of her, sitting back on his heels as he caught his breath — or tried to, anyway. She was on him in a flash, pulling the condom off, slipping her lips back on. Sabine soon had him hard and wanting her all over again. She slid another condom on then pushed him backward, nearly toppling him off the bed so she could straddle him. He knew he was in for the night of his life. With her eyes locked on his and his cock buried deep, she gave him a slow ride. All he could do was stare up at her and think that Sabine-fucking-Cowan was a goddess.

* * * *

He woke up with a sex hangover. His dick was sore, every muscle in his body felt strained — and he was smiling like a madman. *What an unbelievable night.* He shifted, rolling to the side, not really surprised to find himself alone. He pushed himself up on his elbows, noting that the bathroom door was open, the room itself dark. Sabine hadn't stuck around. That wasn't surprising, but, if he were honest, it was disappointing. He collapsed back onto the mattress with a sigh. It wasn't that he was complaining. He'd had an amazing night of hot sex, more times than he'd thought was possible. It had been wild, crazy, uninhibited, no-rules kind of sex in every possible position. Sabine's body and what she could do with it — he moaned at the thought — was like the best porno fantasy times a thousand. *No, times a million.* It was a story for the record books. His friends would likely do just about anything to hear about it. But no one was going to hear about it. That one was locked in the vault, meant for only his enjoyment.

He pulled himself out of bed, making a half-assed attempt to find his clothes, hoping that maybe Sabine was just downstairs getting coffee for them. His phone rang, a muffled sound from across the room. He narrowed his eyes at the pile of clothes, flung haphazardly on the floor. It took him a few seconds to find it, but by the time he did the call had gone to voicemail. There was a text from Roy, a link and nothing else. With a sinking feeling, Trent clicked it.

"Oh fuck," he breathed. The link opened to a popular tabloid where a grainy photo showed Sabine on her knees, looking up at Trent. *"Morgan and Miller Golden Boy Caught with His Pants Down."* There was a spread and a half dozen or more photos. Trent wanted to barf.

Another text came from Roy.

Not good.

Trent closed his eyes briefly, nausea sweeping through him. He typed a response.

I was promised discretion.

It sounded lame. He wanted to take it back the second he pressed Send.
No response.
Fuck. Trent typed.

I'll fix this.

Damage is done. Get your ass back here. I sure as shit hope you got the confidentiality agreement signed.

Trent cursed again. He dug into his pile of clothes, searching for the agreement. He found it crumpled up where he'd left it in the inside pocket of his jacket—unsigned, of course.

His phone dinged again. He looked down, expecting to see another text from Roy, but it was from Sabine.

Had to fly out this morning. Early. Didn't want to wake you.

A second text came.

Had a great time last night. XX See you around.

"Fuck!" Trent threw his phone against the wall, satisfied when it busted to pieces.

Chapter Two

Sabine sat at the small desk on her private jet, airborne and headed to a meeting on the other side of the country. Her thoughts kept drifting to the night before, pulling her from the business proposal she was reviewing.

Trent on his back, staring up at her like she was a goddess riding his dick, his blue eyes zinging with lust and his hands roaming all over her body... He couldn't stop touching her. It had been a while since she'd enjoyed herself like that, an unexpected pleasure and a night of indulgence. Her body trilled at the memory, her nipples hardening, her pussy wet. She adjusted herself, the leather of the seat cushioning her with little resistance. What she could use was some friction. Her clit ached for another round of Trent's cock. He was impressive — and not just because he'd been so eager to pleasure her — but his dick had girth and length, with a wicked bit of a hook that hit her G-spot just the right way.

With a defeated sigh, she shifted the laptop to the side and flipped open the file Adam had given her. *Trent Brooks, twenty-four, graduated from Harvard with distinction, and newly appointed lead communications officer at Morgan and Miller,* the conglomerate that used to include Cowan Enterprises when Sabine's father had been alive. It was run by a group of men whom Sabine had known since she had been a child. They were powerful, arrogant men who didn't know how easily their cocks got them respect, unlike how hard she'd had to work to be taken seriously. They'd each dismissed Sabine's skill as an entrepreneur and hadn't given her the credit she'd deserved, so she'd separated from their corporation and had turned her father's company around, breathing life into something that they'd let fall apart while her father had been ill. But she wasn't one to hold grudges. *Not much anyway.*

Okay, that was a total lie. Her revenge had been silent and steady. Under her direction, Cowan Enterprises was vast and growing. Sex was a lucrative business, both on and off the books. When the power was in the hands of women, it was exponentially more profitable.

Trent Brooks was M & M's golden boy. Sabine had ordered a background check when the chief communications officer, Roy Miller's, secretary had called for an appointment. She'd known Trent inside and out before he'd stepped foot in her home.

Roy's lapdog hadn't come with malicious intent. She'd seen that all over his handsome face. She'd found him amusing, how he'd fumbled through their first meeting. He was young, although at thirty-four, everyone seemed younger than Sabine these days. Not that she had a problem with growing older, even if thirty-five was looming, a milestone that most people from her past thought she'd never make it to. Her good old times had been particularly fun, indulgent and perhaps self-destructive. But she'd come a long way since then. She kept herself in good shape, worked in a bit of Botox here and there for maintenance and generally didn't give a fuck about numbers, unless they were dollars in her bank account.

It'd been a whim to invite him back for the party — partly because she wanted to see his cute dimples again, partly because she wanted to see if she could pump him for information. Even something seemingly benign to him could be useful to her down the road. That was her real business. She was the queen of information. Secrets... Dirty, deadly or otherwise didn't matter. From the lips of the elite to the ears of her girls, everything flowed to Sabine and she kept it all secured in a database that no one would ever get their hands on. She'd taken precautions...extreme ones.

It was unacceptable that those candid photos had been taken. Leaking them to the media could do some serious damage, perhaps more than she was currently anticipating. Her clients were fluttering and tittering about them, and her email was likely already filling up with more concerned inquires. All photos taken at Kitty Call Parties had to be sanctioned by her. Cell phones were strictly forbidden and security was always watching for them. Luckily her clients wouldn't need anything more than a little extra pampering to placate their concerns. The men were easily dealt with.

The fact that the pictures had been so quickly leaked to the press led Sabine to think that Trent was being targeted more than she was, and that had her very curious as to why.

Yesterday afternoon, once Trent had left her office, she'd spontaneously offered him an invite to her exclusive party, sending the message via her right-hand man, Adam, so there were very few people who'd known Trent would be there in the first place. While her world was often rife with controversy, she had to assume that Trent's was not. Either way, the photos wouldn't damage her as much as they would him, and she was feeling uncharacteristically guilty about that — maybe partially because she took pleasure in knowing that a scandal like this would damage the pristine image that Morgan and Miller, a family brand, had worked decades to build. As far as she was concerned, they deserved any negative press that came their way.

Trent was a rising star at the corporation, but he wasn't a bad guy. He'd been working under Roy since he'd been plucked out of the graduation line at Harvard, inventing some of the most influential and innovative PR campaigns that Morgan and Miller had seen in years, making them a relevant household name once again after years of waning sales. Adam's intel had given her a good idea of Trent's background, but none of it gave her any reason to mark him as an enemy. His parents were both alive, living in some buttfuck town in Colorado. They were owners of a butcher shop. He had no siblings and no girlfriend. It was obvious to Sabine that he was married to his job. He had no debt and paid his bills on time. There didn't appear to be any noteworthy vices either, nothing tarnishing his squeaky-clean image.

Sabine didn't have anyone on the inside of M & M. Golden boy with his deadly dimples and sparkling baby blues wasn't going to turn rat. He was too unblemished for that, too enamored of his bosses. She had seen that right away, but it had never been her intention to taint Roy's precious one. If nothing else, she'd figured he'd be a fun ride — and so few men tempted her these days. She'd seen the worst *of* them and therefore always tended to see the worst *in* them. Trent was different — intriguingly youthful, a little naïve and way too trusting. He had a great body under all those clothes. And surprise, surprise, he'd actually cranked her just right, several times, so much so that the thought of him had slicked her pussy with cream all damn day.

M & M also employed one of her now-former clients who, if the rumors were true, had unfortunately overdosed on some prescription meds. CFO Harold McKibbon had had a taste for younger women and a bank account to accommodate his needs. Upon learning of the sudden passing of their chief financial officer, Trent had been immediately dispatched to secure Sabine's signature on a confidentiality agreement to ensure that she wouldn't disclose Harold's extra-marital affairs in a supposed attempt to protect the CFO's wife.

She shifted Trent's profile to the side and looked at a copy of Roy's confidentiality agreement, a ploy if she'd ever seen one. It was pointless for a number of reasons. The CFO's wife didn't need protecting. She already knew all about her husband's dalliances. The thing that Sabine loved the most about her job? Giving power back to women when they were made to feel like they had none. She'd made her fortune on men and their sins, but she refused to do it at the expense of other women if she could help it.

Roy and his business partners were up to something, but she knew they were typical men in all their wickedness and she didn't fear the challenge of finding out what their game really was.

Sabine ran her finger along the side of Trent's photo, distracted once again. "What are your vices? Huh, pretty boy?"

When it came to sex, every move was like a chess game and everyone wanted to get a piece of the queen. Tomorrow, she'd pay a visit to the corporation and step on the game board, see what Morgan and Miller was really after and maybe go another round with her new lover boy. But first she'd have to swallow her pride and admit that there'd been a breach of her security, something that really did piss her off.

"Adam…" She stood from her desk and closed her laptop.

"What's up, boss?" Adam sauntered out of the galley, hand on the butt of his gun as a default.

"I'll be returning to the city this afternoon. Make sure the jet is fuelled and ready when I'm done my meeting."

"You got it." Adam nodded once.

Morgan and Miller's head office was in Midtown East. She had a condo overlooking Central Park that she hadn't been to in quite a while and some private Kitty Call clubs that could use a spot check. There were many reasons to visit New York, but the one that had the most draw and was pumping her up with a surprising jolt of excitement was Trent.

Sabine gave her head a shake and refocused on the wall of oozing sex appeal that was Adam.

"I want the investigation into the photo leak expedited. Spare no expense. Figure out how it happened." Sabine smiled when Adam nodded again. *Such an obedient man. Loyal as fuck. Protective too.* He was also smart with technology and an excellent manager of information. With his bulging muscles and six-foot-three frame, he was total eye candy as well. "Harold

McKibbon is dead." She moved toward him, her eyes locked on his.

Adam gave another nod.

"Send his wife my condolences."

"Already done, boss." Adam's voice was rough. He licked his lips, his gaze trailing from her face to her tits.

Her nipples pulsed. Yes, that was what she needed. A distraction from *him*. She moved within an inch of Adam, her heels putting her at chin level.

Then she hesitated. Adam was *also* not uncharted territory. He was a good fuck, enough to get what she needed when she needed it. But he wasn't Trent. And right now, all she seemed to want was *Trent*.

So she took a step back then another. "I'm tired. I'm going to go lie down in the back." Adam took the hint and stepped toward the galley.

"Tea?" Adam wasn't one of those guys who got possessive. He had carte blanche when it came to the Kitty Cats. His needs were always met and the girls loved him. His loyalty to Sabine was not dependent on their sex life, which was really more about blowing off steam than deepening their relationship. He understood when she needed to focus on other things and he would take a back seat when Sabine devoted herself to someone else...which had happened a time or two over the years.

"I'll have tea later." She rubbed her hand over her eyes, suddenly feeling so beat that all she wanted was to sink into the soft mattress of her bed. "Wake me in an hour."

"You got it, boss." He turned and left her alone.

For a split second she wanted to call him back, to bury her emotions in a familiar routine. But that was just it. Adam had become part of her routine. He wasn't Trent. She wanted to unwrap her new toy and explore the possibilities. Adam didn't make her shiver like Trent had done, and he'd certainly never left her aching like the young communications officer had. Trent was so deliciously intriguing and different.

Her thoughts drifted to the night before and how skillfully Trent had pumped her ass. In the shower, all slippery with soap and water, he'd surprised her with his fat cock slipping and sliding along her crack. When she'd bent over and invited him, he hadn't hesitated. One stroke, wedged in deep, had made her cry out at the fullness and exquisite pressure. He'd pulled her hips back and she'd taken him in to the hilt. He'd snaked his fingers to her clit so that he could rev her up even more. Slow and steady, he'd fucked her until she was once again screaming with pleasure. She'd lost count of the orgasms and had been delirious by the time he'd finally passed out. She liked that he was spontaneous. She loved that he was open to things and that his dick tickled her insides just the right way. She *had* to see him again.

"Fuck me," she sighed. Luckily, she had a drawer full of dildos in the back room. "No rest for the wicked," she mumbled as she moved toward her private suite.

Chapter Three

Trent didn't make mistakes. At least he didn't make gigantically huge, fuck-up-your-life kind of mistakes. It had taken him almost all day to get back to the office. Flight delays and city traffic had all seemed to be working against him, but from the moment he got back from the Hamptons, his life had started unraveling and he couldn't seem to hang on to all the strings.

"The media have been calling all day," Ellie said as she poured him a coffee. "Like, the legit media."

Ellie had been with him for the past few years, pulling all-nighters so that he could pack the punch he needed to impress the higher-ups. She was as driven as he was, set on finishing her business degree. He helped her as much as he could, building a bond that would ensure her loyalty. It was something he'd learned was vitally important in the marketing biz. She'd helped him hit a home run on the last campaign, the one that had given his name meaning—the one that had filled his bank account, and hers too, though to a lesser degree. His value at the company had doubled. No, tripled. And now…this. He couldn't help but feel like he'd let her down too.

A copy of the tabloid that had published the scandalous photos was on Trent's desk. He picked it up and flipped through the two-page spread. "It's bad enough that they got these."

"Roy had a visit from some police this morning." Ellie's tone was hushed.

"Jesus," Trent breathed, dropping the paper then sweeping it off his desk with another curse. Roy's contacts at NYPD wouldn't be too happy that one of his employees had been caught with Sabine Cowan. From what Trent knew, Sabine had been slipping and sliding out of the PD's grasp for her entire life—if not with rumored payoffs from her father when she was into a lot of illegal shit as a teenager, then her more sophisticated brand of evasion that she somehow managed to wield as an adult and entrepreneur. Everyone *knew* that what she did with Cowan Enterprises trespassed into criminal behavior. It was just that no one could actually prove it.

"How did this happen?" Ellie asked, her expression concerned.

"I was—" He gulped back a confession, wanting so badly to admit how stupid he had been. He knew Ellie wouldn't judge him. At least, he hoped she wouldn't. But he couldn't form those words, so instead he said, "I got distracted. I went to get Sab… Ms. Cowan's signature on the paperwork last night and I got caught up in the party."

"Were you drinking?" Ellie took a seat across from him.

Trent shook his head. "Not enough," he mumbled.

"Drugged?" Ellie's voice was hesitant, nudging him toward an excuse that would explain his behavior.

"No."

"Maybe it'll blow over quickly. The legit media outlets probably don't care about Ms. Cowan's antics anymore and no one *really* believes the tabloids." Ellie tried to sound hopeful, but her expression gave her away. He was fucked.

"Yeah... Or maybe someone is trying to destroy my reputation or sully Morgan and Miller and this is going to get worse." Trent sighed. "Fucking stupid. Roy is going to kill me."

"Well, at least you got the confidentiality agreement signed. Roy will appreciate your follow-through on that matter," Ellie said as she stood, ready to leave.

Trent gulped and hung his head. "She didn't sign it." He looked up to meet Ellie's eyes.

"Oh shit!" Ellie whispered, then covered her mouth. "Sorry, I—"

Trent waved her apology away. "I fucked up. Huge."

"Yeah, you did, son." Roy stormed into the room and nodded at Ellie. "Turn the TV on...*Celebrity Beats*."

Ellie jumped to obey.

"I just got off the phone with Sam Henderson. He gave me a heads-up," Roy said, his eyes flicking to the TV that was mounted on the wall.

Trent cursed again, his stomach flipping hard. Henderson was a reporter—a hard-hitting, pull-no-punches kind of reporter. Dangerous. Sometimes he was a friend. Sometimes he wasn't. He liked to exploit controversy.

The TV flared to life, a news report running. Pictures of Trent flashed across the screen. There were shots of him leaving the Cowan mansion, looking disheveled. They had been taken this morning, when he had been frantically trying to get back to the hotel to gather his things. A pretty blonde was speaking. Ellie turned the volume up. *"Trent Brooks, marketing specialist at Morgan and Miller, is no stranger to media attention. Riding high on his new promotion to lead communications officer, playboy Brooks was seen leaving the home of Sabine Cowan this morning, after attending one of her infamous and highly secretive Kitty Cat parties last night."* Another photo flashed across the screen, grainy, taken from a distance, showing Sabine leading Trent up the grand staircase. It wasn't one the tabloid had.

So much for confidentiality. Trent covered his head with his hands. "Fuck me."

"That's bad," Ellie whispered.

"We'd like to warn viewers again that the following video is explicit," the reporter continued.

Trent raised his head. *"What* video?"

The words barely left his mouth when a video popped up, showing him and Sabine in the alcove sunroom. She was on her knees, Trent's head thrown back. The shot had been taken from the doorway, captured by a guest, no doubt. Although it wasn't clear exactly what was going on, no one would question what was happening between him and Sabine.

"Seems that Morgan and Miller's promotional rock star can't keep it in his pants." The screen flipped back to the newsroom, where a male reporter sat snickering a little with the blonde. *"They could be soliciting new business, although I hardly think Cowan Enterprises offers the kind of family entertainment that Morgan and Miller is looking for."*

"Either way, it looks like he's enjoying the perks of his new position," the blonde added.

"Jesus Christ!" Trent jumped up, ready to throw something at the screen.

"Is that slander? Defamation?" Ellie asked.

"It's bad reporting." Roy shook his head. "We can demand a retraction, throw a lawsuit threat their way and see if it does anything."

"The damage is done." Trent sank back into his chair. His parents would see that report. His old professors. Whatever friends he had left.

"What were you thinking?" Roy said as he motioned for Ellie to leave.

She handed him the remote after muting the TV.

Trent shook his head, his world spinning. "I was trying to get her to sign the confidentiality agreement." He watched as Ellie closed the double doors, her eyes shining with pity.

"By sticking your dick in Sabine Cowan?" Roy blurted. "Jesus Christ, Trent!"

"I got caught up in her." Trent threw his hands up. "I can't explain it. She's just so—"

"Bewitching?" Roy suggested as he slumped down into one of the chairs. "I should have warned you, son."

"I've never met a woman like her before," Trent admitted. "She promised that no one would ever find out. She assured me that nothing left Kitty Calls…ever. She seemed so certain of that. That was why she wouldn't sign the agreement. She said that her clients all knew that confidentiality was a guarantee." For fuck's sake, no one knew that Harold had been using her services. *No one except for you.*

"Well, someone didn't get the memo." Roy sighed. "It's only a matter of time before the vultures make the link between Harold and Kitty Calls. What a mess."

"I'm sorry, Roy. It's inexcusable, I know." Trent felt close to tears. He'd worked so hard for what he'd achieved, and it was all hanging in the balance because of an impulse to get his dick wet.

"I've been in damage control all morning and haven't had a chance to speak to anyone else about this," Roy said.

Trent knew that Roy was talking about the other partners. He knew his job was on the line. "I'll turn in my resignation this afternoon."

"Now hang on." Roy pushed himself forward. "Let's not jump the gun here. You fucked up." He pointed a finger at Trent. "Everyone fucks up at some point."

"Not this colossally, though." Trent shook his head. "The pictures alone…"

"You shouldn't have stuck your dick in that whore," Roy spat, then raised his hand. "Sorry. I'm just frustrated." He ran his hand over his face. "Let me talk to the boys, spin this thing a little less against you. You've done well here for us too many times for them to turn their backs on you. And they know Sabine. They know what she's capable of. Trust me. I'll handle it. You should, however, make yourself scarce for a day or two. Come back on Monday." Roy stood.

"Roy," — Trent met Roy's eyes, an act he'd never thought could be so difficult — "I'm truly sorry."

"You sh—"

"Wait! You can't go in there!" Ellie called.

The doors burst open, and with her hands on both doorknobs, Sabine Cowan entered the room.

"Gentlemen." She was wearing a black pencil skirt and a beige silk tank top, with sleek black heels that had to be five inches tall. Her hair was up at the sides, her lips painted impossibly red and her eyes sparkled like she was having the time of her life. "I let myself in."

Roy was out of his seat in a heartbeat, jabbing his finger in the air furiously. "You have some nerve, Sabine!"

Sabine continued into the office, ignoring Roy's anger and instead sauntering over to Trent's bookshelf.

"I tried to stop her, sir," Ellie blathered.

"No, it's fine," Roy lowered his voice, adjusting his tie as he followed Sabine with his eyes. "Close the doors, Ellie, and leave us for a while."

Trent couldn't move. He gripped the sides of his chair, digging his fingers into the leather so hard that he thought he might puncture it. He was pissed that she was there, and he was also riveted to her, his dick hard and aching at just the sight of her curves encased in that skirt, the swell of her tits a hint in the wispy cloth of her top. He twitched at the thought of tracing a line from her waist over her hip as he had done the night before. Her skin was so soft, silky and supple.

"What are you doing here, Ms. Cowan?" Roy had regained control over himself, but his tone still held a hard edge, snapping Trent from his lusty daze.

Sabine glanced over her shoulder, a wry smirk on her lips. "So formal, Mr. Miller? And I thought we were practically family."

"You are like petulant child. Your actions were vicious and inhuman. Again, what are you doing here?" Roy's tone was all venom, like he seemingly had no control where Sabine was concerned. He patted down his tie once more, then turned away from her and headed to Trent's mini bar.

"Well…" Sabine moved toward Trent's desk, her eyes locked on his. "I came here to speak with Mr. Brooks, actually. We have some unfinished business to discuss." She bent down slowly, angling to the side as much as her tight skirt accommodated, to pick up the tabloid that Trent had tossed there. She lifted it, didn't look at it and put it into the trash.

Trent frowned. She wasn't gloating. In fact, the look in her eyes, just for the split second their gazes met, almost seemed —

"Unfinished business?" Roy sputtered. "Oh, I think you finished in a grand way, don't you?" He turned with a glass in his hand, brown liquid sloshing as he pointed toward the TV. "All the media outlets, Sabine! You've ruined him!"

Trent grimaced. A few minutes ago Roy had been saying that his career was salvageable, and now he was ruined? *Ouch.*

"I want you to leave." Trent unclenched his hands from the chair and stood, locking eyes with Sabine. "*Now.* Last night was an error in judgment and I suspect I may have been drugged." The lie tasted bitter, but at the moment, everything felt toxic to him. "I acted out of character and I can't explain my actions otherwise."

"Oh, sweetie," Sabine cooed, "you and I both know that what happened last night was entirely consensual."

"He asked you to leave," Roy said. "I suggest you do that, otherwise I'm sure he can speak to the media about some of the nefarious things he witnessed last night — things that you wouldn't want anyone knowing."

"Oh, like how many times he could make me come? Perhaps how far I squirt? Maybe how long his —"

"Enough!" Roy's face was red again, and he was clenching and unclenching his jaw. "You toy with people's lives, Sabine, and this time you've gone too far. We both know you leaked those photos, that video! For what purpose, I can only assume... Perhaps to get back at me. You and your wild accusations and conspiracy theories."

"Wild accusations? Conspiracy theories? What? Like there isn't a paper trail somewhere of your legal misdeeds as you ran my father's company into the ground while he drooled and withered away in his hospital room? He trusted you *so much*, Roy — so much that he believed you would never do anything to hurt his legacy."

"And here we go, once again your paranoia is rattling around in your muddled brain and puking out of your trashy mouth. There is no paper trail because there were no misdeeds. Your father's company had been struggling for years before he got sick. You were just too busy snorting powder up your nose and posing for nude photos all over the Virgin Islands to notice. As long as your bank account was refilled every time you drained it, what did you care?"

"My father told me, Roy. He told me as he was dying that you were scheming against him. He told me that you couldn't be trusted."

"He told you, did he? When was that exactly? Before or after he started ranting about the little blue dwarfs he insisted were tucking him in at night?"

Sabine's eyes flashed. She came around Trent's desk like she was about to go after Roy with her claws out. Trent intervened, putting himself between her and his boss.

"That's enough." He met her glare, one hand on her wrist, the other on her waist. "You need to leave."

The fire in Sabine's eyes faded quickly and a look of sadness took its place. She opened her mouth as if to say something, her gaze softening even more as she held his stare. Heartbeats passed, silent somethings shining from her eyes. Then she cleared her throat, took a step back and shook off his hold. She walked out without another word, leaving the door open once again.

Roy turned back to pour another drink while Trent quickly moved to the door, watching as Sabine walked away, heading toward the elevators. He had the urge to follow her to demand an explanation. What had that look meant? What words had been left unsaid that had hung between them just then? It was almost like what he'd seen there was regret. But that was probably just wishful thinking.

"She's bad news, boy." Roy was sipping his second round as Trent turned his back to the sight of Sabine and closed the door.

"I know."

"Yes, I believe you do. *Now*." He pointed at Trent, his gaze steady. "Keep your dick and every other part of yourself away from that witch. She's nothing but trouble."

Trouble with a capital T. Yeah, Trent had learned that the hard way and he had no desire to make that mistake again.

Chapter Four

Sabine knew she should have stayed out of the city and let things cool off for Trent. She knew going to Morgan and Miller would only stir the hornet's nest, but that was half the temptation in going anyway. Roy needed a reminder that she still existed and that she still had the power to torment him. The other tempting half had been Trent himself.

Looking only slightly disheveled, with his wild brown curls in disarray, a bit of a scruff on his jaw and his tie hanging undone, he had the expression of a guy who believed he was about to lose it all. Like he'd been fucked—and not in a good way.

So, yeah, she should have stayed away.

But she hadn't.

She'd followed him to the swank bar down the street from his office. It was only just past five, but the place was relatively busy with business deals in progress and dudes in expensive suits booming and blustering their way toward huge gains, or losses, depending on what side of the table they sat.

Trent was at the long mahogany bar, with one hand wrapped around a glass of something brown, the other tapping endlessly against the polished wood, drumming his fingers while he was seemingly deep in thought. He was half-standing, half-leaning against the stool, like he was ready to bolt out of there at any moment. His gaze was riveted to the TV, where an endless loop of scandal was playing. Every ten minutes or so, the images of him and Sabine flashed across the screen and his expression would go from dejection to anger to frustration and back to dejection.

What was hot news right now would die before the end of the day...unless someone fed them something more.

He hadn't noticed when she'd slipped in—and not because the place was perpetually dim, with faux candles and lanterns decorating the place, giving it a strange kind of gothic ambience. He seemed oblivious to everything going on around him, and she did feel bad about that. But not bad enough to leave him be.

She'd wanted to apologize to him back at his office, but Roy's presence had riled her beyond reason. There was no way she'd prostrate herself in front of that old man. And she'd seen something in Trent's eyes, a spark that had told her things weren't dead between them. Not yet, anyway.

No, she was certain he'd give her a chance to talk, that he'd let her in one more time.

She was seated at the back of the bar in a booth, a horseshoe shape that gave her a clear view of Trent from behind as well as in the mirror that lined the back of the bar. His expression was grim once again, his eyes upturned and fixated on the news.

"Can I get you something to drink, ma'am?" The waiter was eyeing her in a familiar way that she was accustomed to. Even though she had her hair up, had donned a large black hat and had kept her sunglasses on, she may have been unrecognizable but she wasn't exactly screaming normal. Celebrities frequented establishments all along this stretch of restaurants and bars, and this place was no different. She didn't want the swarm of attention that usually came her way when she was spotted, and this was not a bar she ever went to, so she was fairly certain the waiter wouldn't be able to place her.

"Sparkling water with lime," she said. "And another round for the gentleman at the bar." She pointed toward Trent.

The waiter looked over his shoulder at Trent then nodded. "Of course — any message for the gentleman?"

"Tell him…" She paused, suddenly stuck for words. What could she say? *Sorry for fucking up your life? Thanks for the good time. Let's do it again?* "Please tell him it's from a friend."

The waiter nodded and left, moving swiftly to do her bidding. She watched with anticipation, her breath catching when Trent accepted the gift, looking slightly confused, a shadow of a smile on his lips as he turned to acknowledge the sender.

He did a double take, squinting into the limited light then widening his eyes as recognition struck.

She offered a smile, trying for it not to come across as predatory, and shifted, welcoming him into her booth with a small wave.

He stood, swayed slightly, took one step in her direction, then turned and walked toward the back hall with not even a glance over his shoulder at her.

Men did *not* turn her down.

She was momentarily stunned. That was not what she was expecting — and it intrigued her even more.

She scooted out of the booth, her pencil skirt making it somewhat difficult to maneuver, and started after him, driven more by the insult than anything else. Could she blame him, though? She was probably the last person he wanted to talk to right now.

The waiter was coming out of the back with her water on a tray. "Is everything all right, ma'am?"

She slipped her fingers into her small purse and pulled out a hundred, neatly folded and ready for such an occasion. "Keep anyone from coming back here." She passed the money to him with a sweep of her fingers against his palm.

"For how long?" He didn't even blink, just took the cash and changed his stance somewhat, shifting so that he could block the pathway behind her.

"As long as it takes," she said. She swept her gigantic hat off and her glasses as she stormed down the narrow hallway and deposited them on a side table outside of the men's washroom.

She didn't knock. She just strode in.

Trent was standing at the sink, gripping either side of the elevated basin. Everything was black marble and cherry wood. A distinct scent of lemongrass and lavender wafted. For a bathroom, it was nice and also very clean.

Trent shifted his eyes to look at her, shock flashing on his face.

"You have some nerve —" he started.

"Honestly, you must know by now that I have a lot of nerve." She waved her hand up in a gesture of 'so what'? "We have things to discuss."

"Here?"

She smiled at his expression. "Well, you snubbed me out there."

"I don't want to be seen with you. My reputation is already in the gutter. Can you imagine what the press would do if they saw me with you again? You ruined me." He turned to face her fully. "Sabine—"

The door behind her opened and the waiter poked his head in. "Um, ma'am, I didn't know you were headed in here. It's against policy—"

"Leave us!" she commanded, turning on her heel to face the waiter. "Now!"

The waiter's face paled and recognition dawned. "Of course, Ms. Cowan, anything you want. I-I-I'll guard the door—"

"Get out!"

He stammered a bit more then did as he'd been told. She flicked the lock once the door was closed, something she should have done when she'd first entered.

"That's what you're used to, right? Everyone bowing down to the infamous Sabine Cowan?" Trent's voice rose.

She turned to face him. "Yes," she said simply.

"And you expect me to just accept what you've done?" He pointed to the door. "You know that guy. He's out there right now texting all his buddies that Sabine fucking Cowan is in the men's bathroom at the Crown and Fig. They'll be down here in five minutes flat...and so will the media. Haven't you done enough damage already?"

Her confidence wavered slightly, an unusual feeling for her. She probably should have just left him alone. "I won't let that happen." But even she didn't completely believe her words.

"Oh, really? You won't?" he scoffed. "The damage is done, Sabine, and now it's just going to get worse. Now I'm going to get fired for sure. I barely made it out of there today with my job."

He turned away from her to resume his position at the sink, his shoulders tense and hands gripping the basin as if he'd fall over if he didn't. She moved toward him tentatively, like she was approaching a skittish animal.

"Trent," she whispered. "I'm not going to let anything bad happen—"

He glared at her as he turned, taking her by surprise when he grabbed her waist and pulled her toward him. "Shut up!"

And he crushed his lips to hers. It was a punishingly brutal kiss that took her breath away with its ferocity, his grip on her waist tightening as he pulled her closer.

He slammed her back so she hit the edge of the sink with a thump, the dampness from the sink soaking through her skirt instantly, but his lips never left hers. His hands were like vise grips and his dick, rock hard and jutting against his pants, stabbed against her repeatedly. She let her purse drop to the counter and lifted her hands to his hair, holding him tightly as he bit and licked and stroked her mouth and tongue, matching him thrust for thrust.

Her body coiled with excitement and anticipation, her pussy clenching, aching for his dick to slide in deep. Bracing herself against the counter, she took every bit of his aggression, every nip of his teeth, every grunt of his frustration.

He didn't stop, the urgency of his movements telling her just how much he wanted to sink into her too. His groans of anguish or pleasure were indistinguishable. He wanted her but he didn't want her—a battle she knew so well.

She moved her hand to the back of her skirt and managed to unzip herself just as Trent pulled away, his eyes wild. He raised his hands like he'd been touching something he shouldn't.

"*You* do this to me!" he said, his words frenzied and desperate sounding.

She locked eyes with him and nodded, then let her skirt drop to the floor.

He registered it with a flick of his gaze, nothing more than that, but his restraint was clearly costing him. His clenched jaw was a signal that he was holding back, reining in his desire...but not by much.

She was bare, as usual, with no panties and nothing barring him from her pussy except for his own clothes. She reached her fingers down and stroked herself, dipping into her folds until they were coated in cream. She lifted them so he could see, so he could smell. Her arousal was slicked down her finger. She was wet as fuck for this man.

He was panting, hard, almost like he was out of breath, when really, she knew, he was trying to reel himself in, keep himself under control.

She smiled, wickedly, like a predator taunting its prey.

With a flick of her tongue, she sucked her fingers into her mouth, pumping like she would him, envisioning the things she's like to do to his cock, sucking, laving, flicking, tasting her own cream and making herself wetter, if that were possible. And all the while she kept her eyes locked on his, watching for that moment — that moment that showed her his resolve was slipping, that he just couldn't take it any —

He grabbed her hip with one hand while unzipping himself with the other. It all took a matter of seconds before he'd lifted her completely, hoisting her up for her to wrap her legs around his waist so he could sheath his dick completely in her hot and pulsing pussy.

He groaned, sliding his eyes shut. She moaned, watching him so that when he opened his eyes again, he could see just how much she wanted — no, *needed* — this. And when he did, his eyes flashing as he locked on hers, he groaned again, seemingly realizing just how right it was, just how much they both needed this.

He moved them, slamming her up against the door so that she cried out with a mixture of pain and pleasure. Then he pummeled her hard and fast, brutal in his need to fuck her, digging his fingers into her flesh, enough so they'd leave bruises. He didn't look away, kept his eyes focused on hers, unapologetically locked in and screaming with intensity.

She had her hands in his hair, holding him tight as he pumped her again and again, his balls slapping her ass with each thrust, his cock grinding against her clit, hurting almost unbearably as her piercing abraded her skin.

"Yes," she moaned, closing her eyes.

"No!" he growled. "Look at me. Look at what you do to me!"

She saw there, in his eyes, the lust she felt for him shining back at her. Her orgasm rose swiftly, her pussy clenching hard as a wave of pleasure ran down her spine and through her body. It was too good...too powerful.

"Fuck!" she screamed as she exploded, milking him as he continued to slam into her, his dick growing even more rigid, punishing her over and over until he apparently couldn't do it anymore, his own climax bursting deep inside, soaking her with his cum, hot jets that she could feel as he pumped and pumped inside her.

She wrung him dry, taking all that he had to offer, moving with him as his thrusts slowed and his body began to slump, the tension there sliding away. Her own body felt languid, like she wouldn't be able to stand if he put her down right this moment.

"Trent," she whispered, moving her hands from his hair to the sides of his face. "I'm so—"

Bang! Bang! Bang!

The door vibrated behind them.

"This isn't a brothel, Ms. Cowan!" a booming male voice yelled. "I will *not* have my establishment sullied in this way!"

Trent's eyes flashed with anger then with panic. He froze. She could see the word 'fuck' echoing through his thoughts.

The owner tried to open the door. The flimsy lock barely held.

"You will *not* come in here," Sabine called loudly. The rattling of the knob stopped. It would buy her only moments, she knew.

"Trent, it'll be okay." Sabine coaxed him to let her down, his dick sliding from her pussy. "Can you get my skirt?" she said softly, pointed toward the puddle of black cloth on the floor.

He nodded, and as he turned away, Sabine closed her eyes, sucked in a deep breath and counted to five, reining in her temper at the racket that the owner was making on the other side of the door. She caught snippets of words she'd heard a million times before. *Whore. Dilettante. Shameful. Slut.*

Trent brought her the skirt, flickering his gaze to the door, looking like he was about to face a firing squad.

She donned her clothes quickly and did her best to straighten herself, then grabbed her purse and her phone.

She texted Adam.

Bathroom. Back hall.

Of course Adam was close by. He always was. But she'd told him not to interfere unless she asked. He would follow the crowd though, and there was most definitely a crowd growing.

"What—?" Trent started.

"I'll take care of this. Trust me," she said as she leaned up and kissed Trent gently. He looked bewildered, which she thought was cute. He was a little dazed from their intense fucking, but also probably on the verge of a full-on panic attack.

Right outside, Adam texted back. But he hadn't needed to—his voice was clear on the other side of the door.

"Ms. Cowan isn't taking any questions at this time. Move back, people."

"Stay here for a full minute after I leave, okay? Don't go anywhere without Adam."

"Adam?"

"My bodyguard. He'll take care of you."

Trent's eyes were wide, darting from her to the door like he was getting ready to bolt.

She reached up and grabbed the sides of his face, steadying him. "A full minute, Trent."

She forced him to nod.

"Sab—"

She cut him off with another tender kiss then let his face go and slipped out of the door. Flashes went off immediately, the din of a thousand questions rising almost at once.

"I will have you know, Ms. Cowan, that I do not abide—"

She turned on the owner, her fury unleashed. "And I will have *you* know that your women's washroom is in a deplorable state and I was forced to use the men's as the only alternative available. Do you think so poorly of your female patrons that…" As she continued to blast him, a bevy of lies coming out of her mouth, Adam moved behind her, slipping into the men's washroom in order to direct Trent.

She kept the crowd moving backward as she accosted the owner. "Not to mention, this is the twenty-first century. There are such things as universal washrooms. I'm not obligated to abide by your ridiculously sexist notions of privacy."

"We heard—"

"You heard what exactly?" Sabine snapped, a challenge for this man to voice his accusations in front of the camera and further sully his bar's reputation. "I'm certain, Mr.…."

"McKean."

"Mr. McKean, that what you heard was a woman trying to use the facilities with some degree of privacy before the media descended on her. Is this how you normally conduct business, sir? Your wait staff informing the media when a celebrity is trying to use the washroom? I'd hate to imagine what would happen if word got out that discretion is not at the top of your priorities when it comes to your patrons."

"That's not..." Mr. McKean's eyes were wide, darting back and forth from her to the press of media around them. "I had no idea, Ms. Cowan. P-please accept m-my apologies," he stammered.

"And you all, looking for a story already? Don't you have enough to write about these days?" She addressed the reporters, who were shifting backward as she pushed forward, moving out to the main pub, causing more of a stir among the patrons who were still seated.

"Ms. Cowan, what do you have to say about the recent video that shows you..."

And so it went. She moved herself out of the pub altogether, pulling the media away from Trent completely so that Adam could get him out of the back door, with everyone none the wiser. It meant being hounded by the press for longer than she liked, dodging their ridiculously intrusive questions and giving them a bit of a tease with an announcement regarding one of her lingerie lines, but it gave Adam enough time to do what needed to be done.

She felt the vibration, two quick buzzes on her phone to let her know that Trent was out. She didn't even need to look to know Adam had done his job. He always did his job. He'd take care of the waiter as well, making sure that his phone, which likely had photos, was dealt with. The last thing she needed, more so for Trent than her, was another leak.

She was exhausted by the time it was over. She loathed the media, especially since they thrived on her life like piranha or sharks. Despite her hatred of them, she knew their tricks and how predictably they'd react to a situation. She was the draw, and a word with her was more important than whatever or whoever had been behind the bathroom door. Pulling them away from Trent was the least she could do, even if it cost her energy and time she didn't really have.

Trent isn't going to get fired today — not because of me, anyway.

Chapter Five

He did everything he could to keep the shit-eating grin from his face while he was at work. It was a hard thing to do when Sabine Cowan was sending tantalizing texts all the damn day. The woman knew just how to crank him up.

Did you know I can come just by stimulating my nipples?

No, I wasn't aware. Fascinating.

Yeah, I'll show you tonight. You can put some chocolate sauce on my nips and suck them until I explode.

You're killing me.

Is your dick hard?

Yes.

Super hard?

Yes.

We'll put some chocolate sauce on that too. I'll bring an extra bottle.

"You're grinning at your phone again," Ellie said, her voice a whisper. "Give it to me until the meeting is over."

They were riding in the company car, on their way to a meeting with an important distributor. They were hashing out a series of commercials that would partner up the two mega-companies. They had been Trent's idea that Roy had given him the green light to pursue — after, of course, securing permission from the other partners. They weren't happy with the media fiasco that had occurred, but in the weeks that had passed, the focus on him and Sabine had died to almost nothing. As long as he kept his head in the game — and his relationship with Sabine on the down-low — he might just survive the whole ordeal.

And Sabine was being extra cautious, making sure that they were never seen together, picking him up unexpectedly as he'd exited the subway, her limo's darkened windows concealing what they were up to.

'Hey, sexy, wanna lift?' Sabine had had the window rolled down, her face partially concealed behind one of those big hats she liked to wear.

The first time she'd propositioned him had been the day after they'd fucked in the Crown and Fig's bathroom. Even though he'd been still stressed out about the whole thing, he did understand the sacrifice she'd made to protect him.

He'd gotten into her limo, honestly thinking she was going to give him a lift. *How naïve, right?*

The second he'd slipped inside, she was on him — kissing him fiercely, demanding with her body that he respond the same way. It was like everything was forgotten. His mind had definitely forgotten anyway, what with her lips on his cock and her tits spilling from her dress to distract him.

He'd had her legs over his shoulders, his hands on her hips, drilling her sweet pussy in the time it took them to travel less than a block.

And that was how it had gone almost every day since.

Quick fucks on the leather seats of her car, the driver keeping the partition closed and somehow ignoring the grunting and moaning coming from behind him. Or maybe he wasn't ignoring it... Trent didn't actually care, because sinking his dick deep into Sabine's pussy was all he could think about, leaving him in a weird kind of satiated limbo where he experienced only momentary relief from his ever-present, Sabine-inspired hard-on as he spilled cum into her then got dropped off a block or two away in a daze. It was satisfying up to a point. He wanted to spend more time with her but wasn't sure how that would happen with things as they were. He understood how addiction worked, and he knew he was developing a serious one for Sabine and her glorious pussy.

Trent slipped his phone into his jacket pocket. "You're right. I'm distracted. I won't check texts again until we're done."

"You know how important this deal is," Ellie reminded him.

Trent nodded. Yeah, he knew. It was more important than anything else, even Sabine, in this moment. It meant his career and was the ultimate deciding factor in whether or not Morgan and Miller kept him on. It was a test. Roy hadn't said as much, but the message was clear. *Fuck this up and you're out.* And Trent had worked too damn hard to get his career to this point to lose his grip at this stage.

So he wouldn't be fucking it up, but he also wouldn't be ending things with Sabine either. She was just too...intoxicating. He wanted the best of both worlds and he believed he could ultimately have it all. And why not? It was just sex and business, right? All powerful men had their vices, Roy included. Sabine was his vice...a tantalizingly sexy, hot as fuck vice that he really couldn't give up.

"I'm sorry. I'm not your mother, but here I am acting like one." Ellie laughed with a note of discomfort. "How are you doing, anyway?"

Trent gave her a warm smile. "Great, fine... I'm doing fine."

"Good." Ellie smiled back, a blush on her cheeks. "All that nasty business with that awful woman... She could have destroyed—"

"Hey, let's go over the storyboard one more time, okay?"

Ellie immediately clamped her mouth shut and shifted to business mode, her full attention back in the game.

And that was what the last few weeks had been like for Trent. People wanted to talk about it, to lecture about it, to remind Trent just how close he'd come to a colossal fuck up—his parents, his bosses, even his secretary. The only people who seemed to get it were his buddies, and even they were crude and rude about the whole thing, wanting to know the dirty details of his hook-up with Sabine. *If they only knew.*

But keeping Sabine a secret was half the fun. The danger of that alone? *Whew...exhilarating.*

The car slowed, Ellie shuffled the boards back together. Everything looked great.

"You ready?" Trent breathed out the words. He'd pitched the concept weeks ago to the CEO of Franklin Spec, a company that specialized in baby monitors. Morgan and Miller had been trying to secure a connection with the company for years but so far hadn't been able to make it work. It had been Trent's idea to use M&M's flawless track record of reliable safety products, coupled with the renewed power behind the household name. Franklin Spec would be foolish to turn down the deal. Trent had worked with the best team available, a cranked-up group of artists and commercial creatives who really got what Trent was trying to do. It was a bit edgy, sure, but hard-hitting had seemed to work for Morgan and Miller on the last campaign, so Trent was confident it would work again. It all hinged on how the meeting went today.

"I'm ready. Let's do this, boss," Ellie said, her eyes sparkling with enthusiasm.

Trent adjusted his tie, then followed her out of the car and into the building, ready to pitch the hell out of his commercial series.

* * * *

And they hated it.

Okay...'hate' was a strong word.

They liked parts of it, in a lukewarm kind of way.

The message was too dark. Too focused on fearmongering. Franklin Spec wasn't interested in that approach. Not really, anyway. They wanted a more positive spin. They wanted him to flip the entire thing on its head — and they wanted it by the next day or the deal was off.

He'd texted Sabine and canceled their plans, which disappointed him, sure, but was a sacrifice she seemed to understand. *'Take care of business,'* she'd said.

And after hours of working on the new pitch, they only had a rough idea in place. Trent was dreading approaching the creative team with it in the morning. He'd be asking them for a fucking miracle. They were good, but were they *that* good? He wasn't so sure. He had to do better, to bring them something more concrete.

He rubbed his eyes, feeling the burn of too many hours spent staring at the screen.

"You should go home," he said to Ellie.

Her eyes were puffy and red, and she squinted every time she looked at her computer screen.

"What? No! We're not done!" But midway through her protest, she yawned.

"Seriously, Ellie, go home. I'll finish typing up this version. It's not like another hour is going to make a difference on the quality. Let me keep mulling this over. Something will come to me...probably." He gave her a lopsided grin that he knew would disarm her.

She closed her computer. "You sure?"

She'd stay if he asked her to.

Trent nodded. "Yeah, get some sleep. We have a long day ahead of us and you're way better with organizing stuff anyway. I'll need your brain at full capacity in the morning."

"I messaged Steve. He'll be ready for your ideas early, and I'll come back before six." She nodded to the couch. "I put some clean sheets in the closet. Do you want me to make up the couch? I know you're not going home tonight."

"Nah, I can do it."

She yawned again. "I'll stop by the dry cleaner and pick up your other suit and a new shirt—the soft blue one that shows off your eyes." She shrugged. "Can't hurt."

Trent chuckled. "Thanks, Ellie. You're the best."

She waved him off as she walked out of his office. "Oh, I didn't see you there. Yes, of course." She poked her head back in. "The custodian is here to clean up. Are you okay with that?"

Trent barely looked up from his computer, his fingers flying across the keys. "Yeah, sure, send him in."

He was scrolling through the document. It wasn't his best work. His best work was sitting in the trash on his computer, discarded after the owner of Franklin Spec had pulled him aside and told him that there would only be a merger if Trent could produce something that highlighted the complete values of the company. He'd stressed the word 'values', sending a message to Trent that he knew damn well what had gone down with Sabine Cowan and that he disapproved. It made Trent bristle, partly because he was sick of the judgment heaped on Sabine and partly because his idea was a damn good one—even Roy thought so—but it was too risky for Franklin. He had to wonder if it would have gone over better before the Sabine controversy.

But, Trent had something to prove, again, and he wasn't the kind of guy to turn down a challenge, so he was willing to bend to Franklin's wishes.

He and Ellie had come up with a new idea, sure, and it wasn't a terrible one. It just wasn't going to pack the punch that M&M was used to from Trent. And he did have a reputation to salvage.

The custodian wheeled in a cart in that looked loaded with rags or something. Trent glanced up and nodded then returned to his work. There had to be an angle he wasn't seeing…

He kept skipping over the same block of text. At the rate he was going, he'd probably go cross-eyed by the end of the night. And fuck, his head was starting to hurt from the glare.

He sucked in a deep breath. Maybe Ellie was right. Maybe it was time to pack it in. He leaned back, stretching his arms over his head, stifling a groan that might sound weird to the custodian. The air shifted and Trent caught the scent of something different.

"What's that smell?" Trent inhaled deeply. All of a sudden it kind of smelled like… "Roasted chicken?"

He looked over at the custodian, who was busy dusting the bookshelf.

Trent frowned.

Busy dusting the bookshelf?

The guy had his back to Trent. He was short and chunky, his gray uniform bulking out in a way that said too many beers and wings on too many nights. His black hair was scraggly looking and hung in uneven clumps to his collar. He had a baseball cap on that Trent knew wasn't company issue and a feather duster in his hand that was so old school and unusual looking…

"Um…you're new here, aren't you?"

Trent stood up, pushing his chair back, the hairs on the back of his neck rising. They'd had a spy infiltrate before, according to Roy. It had been competition trying to get company secrets and, once, even an activist who had been convinced that Morgan and Miller was trafficking sex workers or something.

The custodian froze mid swipe. His baseball cap obscured his face and he was obviously trying to keep from turning toward Trent. Something was definitely up. Trent clenched his fists. Even though the custodian had at least a hundred pounds on him, Trent was sure he wouldn't have a problem taking the guy down. *Probably.*

"Let me see your ID."

What he should have been doing was calling security. Trent reached toward his phone just as the guy started to turn, moving his hand to his pocket.

"Hold it—"

The custodian turned, whipping off his hat at the same time. A cascade of blonde hair fell free and Trent gasped, his heart hammering from the adrenaline of it all.

"Sabine?"

"Did I freak you out? 'Cause you look totally freaked out right now." She patted down her bulky body. "Do you like it?" She pouted. "Does it make me look fat?"

Trent moved around his desk, trying to keep his heart under control. Okay, yeah, she'd totally freaked him out. For a minute there he'd thought maybe the custodian was gonna pull a gun.

"You look funny." He pulled her into his arms — somewhat difficult with all the bulk — and kissed her. "But also strangely sexy."

"I fooled you though, right?" She was grinning as she kissed him again.

Her breath smelled of berries, and she tasted like she always did, delicious.

"Yeah, you got me." He patted her ass, which was also padded with stuffing of some sort. "Where'd you get the costume?" Then he added, "You didn't tie up the usual custodian, did you? Lock him in a closet?"

She ran her hands up his torso before pulling away. "Nah, I just threw him a few bills and told him to take the night off. I brought you dinner." With another kiss she extracted herself from his grip. "You're hungry, right?"

She moved over to the cart and started pulling the rags off the top.

"So that's why I smelled chicken." He followed her over, getting the full aroma of whatever she'd brought. "I already had dinner." His stomach growled loudly.

Sabine cocked an eyebrow and continued to move things around, pulling out a covered plate and handing it to him before reaching inside for another.

"Okay, I can eat," Trent said. He took the two plates from her and walked over to his desk. "What about security? Did they see you come in?"

"Adam dealt with security…"

"Dealt with like…how?"

She rolled her eyes as she pulled out a bottle of wine. "Your security dude and Adam are old buddies from way back. He turned the other way when we came in." She set two glasses on his desk then handed him a corkscrew and the bottle. "Don't worry… No one knows I'm here."

"You're full of surprises." Trent twisted in the corkscrew and worked the cork out. "I love that you're here, but I can only take a break for a few minutes." He nodded toward his computer. "I'm not happy with what I've got so far."

Sabine stopped her fussing with the utensils and looked up, her brow furrowed. "You can't work all night. It's not good for your brain."

He sighed as he poured the wine. "I know, but I've got to hit this one out of the park again or I'm gonna get cut from the team."

Sabine picked up her glass and took a sip, then walked around his desk, motioning him out of the way as she nudged his seat back to accommodate her girth. His cursor was blinking, waiting for the next line of text. "Can I look?" She was still wearing the ridiculous fat suit but didn't seem to mind that it made her waddle a little. She slumped down in his chair and swiped her finger across the track pad.

Trent nodded then shrugged, accepting that food would do him good. He moved to the opposite side and picked up his plate. He really was starving now that there was something more edible in front of him. Ellie had gotten them subs, but that had been hours before. Sabine had brought a full meal — half a chicken, roasted potatoes, green beans and a roll. The smell alone was making him drool. "Mind if I eat?"

She waved him on as she concentrated on the screen, her fingers moving as she scrolled through his work.

After about ten minutes of her not saying anything and him devouring everything on his plate, he leaned against the side of the desk, watching her read, her brow still furrowed as her eyes flicked back and forth across the screen.

"It's bad, right?" He sighed.

She shifted her eyes up to his. "Was the food good?"

She moved her chair closer to him, closing the laptop screen as she did. She moved her fingers to the buttons on her shirt, fluttering her eyelashes as she looked up at him.

"The food was good, but I have to—"

Her shirt didn't have buttons, Trent realized. It was closed with Velcro, and as Sabine pulled it apart, Trent saw that she was naked underneath.

"Ah, so the suit itself is padded?"

She smirked and nodded, her tits swaying as she pushed her chair closer.

His dick strained against his pants. God, he wanted this. He wanted to suck on her tits and sink into her pussy, but he couldn't. He tore his eyes away and glanced at his computer.

"I really have to—"

"No, Trent, this just won't do." She pushed her chair back abruptly and stood. "I can't have you worrying about work right now, not when I'm here to relieve your stress."

"Sabine, I'm sorry. I just can't risk losing this deal."

"I know. I get it…" But she kept moving, going to the cart and grabbing something. "But you need a break. Trust me. The best ideas come at the weirdest times—and always when you're not focusing on them. Let me distract you for a bit, get your mind on other things."

Trent sighed. He so badly wanted to give in.

She came up behind him just as he was about to stand and slipped a cloth over his eyes.

Trent turned toward her, lifting his hand as if to remove the blindfold. But she stopped him with a soft touch. Her lips were at his ear, the feel of her breasts brushing against his chest a tease through his shirt. "Trust me, baby. I'm going to make you feel so good that the ideas will just start pouring out of you."

His dick pulsed. She unzipped his pants and palmed his aching cock.

"Let me take care of you, baby," she purred.

Chapter Six

He was way too tense—too tense to work, too tense to think. Sabine had found that a good fuck was all she usually needed to get the creative juices flowing—or *some* kind of juices flowing. What he needed was a big release.

She moved him to his desk chair, one of those leather monstrosities that were supposed to be good for posture or something. She rarely did work at a desk, and if she did, it wasn't long enough to cause back strain. But his chair was perfect for her needs. He didn't take the blindfold off, which was good, because she suspected he had some control issues, wanted to follow the rules but was always tempted to break them. She could sense it, a constant battle waging between proper gentlemanly behavior and the alpha within. Trent's aggression was there, just under the surface of his calm and collected demeanor. Although she loved that he was willing to play with her, she wanted to see if she could unleash his dominant side. Dimples or not, Trent was all power and sex appeal. There was nothing school-boy innocent about him, not deep down anyway.

She pulled out the rope she'd brought in her cart and used it to bind his wrists to the chair arms.

"What are you—?"

"Nah-ah, this is my game tonight. I get to call the shots."

"Don't you call the shots every night?" Trent sighed his resignation as he slumped farther into the chair. "Maybe you should lock the door."

Good idea…but she didn't, and she wasn't going to. The threat of getting caught made her wet, even if the actual threat of getting caught was nil. The building was empty and even if there were a minute risk, Adam would make sure that no one got to their floor.

Once Trent was secured, the bonds tied as tight as she could make them without causing him too much pain, she stripped down to nothing. The fat suit was bulky but light, and it hadn't caused her to overheat, but she was happy to be rid of it. She preferred being naked anyway. The cool air against her skin, the cushion of the carpet under her feet, the leather of the chair that brushed her thigh…

"Baby," she whispered against his ear, making sure her tits rubbed the back of his hand before she climbed onto his lap. She licked along the seam of his lips, coaxing him to open his mouth so she could suck on his tongue. She moved her hands to open his pants wide, pulling his cock out to stroke it as she plundered his mouth, nipping his bottom lip until he grunted.

His cock was weeping for her. She rubbed his precum over his crown. "I'm going to suck you, baby, hard and long, until you come in my mouth. Then I'm going to ride you. I'm going to squeeze every last drop from your cock. But first, I'm going to make you beg for it."

She wrapped her hand around his shaft and pumped him, taking him from tip to base over and over again, cupping his balls and squeezing lightly before stroking him again. The salty taste of him filled her mouth and his girth stretched her lips. She really wanted to make him come, but as soon as he started bucking into her, his hips rising off the chair, she stopped, disentangled herself and stepped away.

He groaned. "Don't stop."

"My game tonight," she said. She pulled out her toolkit. It was a little box she'd packed so she could play a bit with Trent's thresholds.

She picked up her feather duster and a small leather whip. They'd talked and teased a bit about pain and pleasure over the last few weeks, enough for Sabine to know that Trent wasn't opposed to the idea. She just wasn't entirely sure how far he'd go—or how much control he could tolerate giving up. She was used to being in a position of power, especially in the bedroom. If he turned out to be a total sub, she could work with that.

"Sabine..." he groaned.

She grinned. She did like that tone. It gave her chills when a man begged her for release. It was one of her favorite things to hear. That and the moan of pleasure when she finally let him come. She rubbed her clit with the end of the whip handle, stroking herself a little. *Mm-m-m, yes...* She could keep another slave if things worked out that way.

She fluttered the feather duster over the length of his dick.

He opened his mouth to question her, no doubt, then yelped instead when she brought the whip down against his flesh with a light slap. His dick bobbed.

"Remember that time we talked all night on the phone?" It had been like she was a teenager again and couldn't get enough of hearing his voice. They'd regretted it the next day, both acting like zombies at their respective jobs, but it'd been worth it. She hadn't giggled that much in years. Maybe that was what she loved the most about Trent, his youthful approach to everything. He was filled with so much energy and excitement, even toward her, like she was this conquest he was determined to have—like she was something special and not the Queen of Smut that most people looked down their noses at. Maybe it was a celebrity fetish of his, but his enthusiasm was infectious and he really did make her feel like she was worth every minute of his time.

"I-I-I d-do remember."

She liked his stutter. It made her smile and her heart warm in a curious way.

She shook her head then continued with her task.

Rolling the feather duster around the girth of his cock, she spent some time caressing his balls then leaned so she could lick his ear lobe, sucking for a bit. The moans she pulled from him made her shiver, a jolt straight down her spine.

He was writhing now, shifting in his seat, his muscles straining against the bonds.

"That feels fucking good," he said, "but I want your pussy on my dick."

There it was…that tone that made her think he had a Dom in him. It was guttural and deep, like he was just at the point of commanding her.

She pulled away again, playing for a little longer with the feather duster while she slowly unbuttoned his shirt. She ran the feather duster's handle up his torso, circling his nipples until they were hard little nubs.

"Remember what I told you about pain?"

She brought the whip down again, smacking the tip of his cock with more force than before.

"Yes," he groaned, throwing his head back and gritting his teeth as she struck him again—and again. His cock was red where she'd lashed him.

"Say it," she ordered.

"Pain is a state of mind," he growled, his teeth still clenched, gripping the arms of the chair with his hands.

"And?"

She whipped harder, making sure that the tips of the whip hit his balls.

He hissed. "It's totally in my control," he said on a burst of breath.

She smacked him one more time, smiling at the uniformly rosy red that was rising to the surface of his skin.

She got on her knees and rubbed her cheek against his flesh, noting the nice heat there.

"Mm-m-m." She slipped her lips over his dick, sucking away the lingering burn she'd raised, slurping up the spurt of precum that hit the inside of her cheek.

Trent was moaning too, and bucking once again.

"Yes, yes, don't stop… Don't—" He groaned when she popped her lips off of him.

"Not yet, cowboy." She gripped the end of his cock and applied pressure, enough to stop him from coming. It was a nice little torture trick she'd discovered in her younger years, tried and tested many times.

"What are you doing?" he moaned, shifting his head this way and that, bucking his hips like a wild man.

She released him and stepped away. He jolted, his dick questing for her touch.

"Sabine…."

"Are you begging me, big boy?" She climbed on top of him, making sure that her body didn't actually touch any part of his exposed flesh. Her legs were straddling his and her pussy, throbbing with intensity from the thrill of the tease, was hovering high enough that he couldn't touch her. Her tits swayed just at his chest. She gripped his arms and leaned as close as she dared. "If you want me, you know what to say."

"Sabine… I…" He growled. "I…" He gritted his teeth, clenching his jaw once again.

She laughed. "Not ready to say it, eh?"

He moaned when she rubbed her nipples along his chest and pressed her lips to his jaw.

"Just say it, baby," she purred.

But he didn't—and that was a green light for her next move. She leaned over the side of the chair and hit the release so that it reclined farther, putting him at the perfect angle, not quite horizontal but close enough.

Her pussy was so slick, dripping with cream. She moved her hand to his dick, adjusting her stance so that she could part her pussy lips enough to encase his shaft, leaning forward so that rock-hardness was pressed to his stomach.

He groaned loudly. "What are you doing to me now?"

But she just laughed again and rubbed herself against his dick, moving just a tiny bit so that her pussy slid up then down his length.

"You want me, big boy?" she purred.

She slid down until she was gliding so low that she felt his balls and used the angle to lick and suck on his nipples, circling the hard little buds with her tongue, nipping before soothing the bite with another round of tongue attention.

He was writhing. She encased him again, moving along his shaft with her sopping wet pussy. Her body ached for him. Her tits felt heavy, her nipples pulsing with heat and pressure. She was almost at the brink of giving in herself, wanting his hands on her, having his lips take possession and his dick wedged in deep.

"Say it, Trent. Say it and I'm all yours."

He grunted, moving his hips to push against her with urgency. She quickly lifted up and used her technique, pinching the tip of his cock to stop him from coming.

He cried out this time, his whole body heaved and the chair lurched.

"You're a filthy, dirty tease, woman. Untie me now so I can punish your cunt!" he bellowed.

Sabine giggled, giddy at the switch she'd flipped. She jumped off Trent and released only one of his hands, giving herself enough time to get away before he got to her. But she didn't have long, because with another bellow, he tore his other hand free and wiped off the blindfold. His face was set with a look of pure aggression that made her shiver with excitement.

She made it to the other side of the office when he caught her, his movements a frenzy of power. He latched on to her arm, yanking her back against his chest, her wrist captured tightly in his grip.

"You're not going anywhere," he growled against her throat, scraping her skin with his teeth and sending a chill down her body.

She moaned when he captured her tit with one hand, cupping her roughly, her nipple slipping between his fingers so he could pinch and pull at her aching peaks.

"I'm going to make you beg, *baby*," he said, "but not tonight."

He moved his other hand to her pussy, slipping his fingers deep inside and rubbing along her clit.

"Tonight I'm going to fuck your brains out."

He pushed her to the floor, moving with her, his fingers still inside, pumping her, teasing her. She was bucking and moaning and gritting her teeth. Her pussy was so slick that she could feel it dripping with each swipe he made. He flicked and twisted her nipple, rubbing his palm over to soothe the burn before doing it again.

With her ass in the air and his body draped over her, he moved his fingers out and replaced them with his dick. He began hard, pounding thrusts that moved her knees on the carpet, giving her an instant burn, but she didn't dare move or ask him to stop. No, she took it. His hips ground against her ass, his balls slapping in his frenzy. He bellowed his release, her own climax mounting seconds after, his cum scorching her with a delicious heat.

He pulled out and stood, picking her up by the waist and carrying her to the couch like she weighed nothing, then throwing her down so she was splayed and breathless.

His eyes were predatory, hungry.

There's the aggression, the power!

His cum was dripping from her pussy and he watched as she slipped her fingers down to capture some.

"Taste it," he ordered.

She lifted her fingers to her lips and sucked them in, taking his cum down her throat and moaning to let him know just how much she loved it.

Then he was on her again, his cock wedged in deep and tight. With her legs over his shoulders and him holding her tits, he fucked her brains out.

* * * *

She left him asleep on the couch, putting herself back in her disguise so she could slip out with no one the wiser. He was totally out of it, exhausted to the point of oblivion. She kissed him on the forehead and was smiling as she left.

He'd no doubt wake up in a panic come morning, thinking he was fucked — and not in a good way — with his proposal, but she'd left something for him to read that she knew would carry his idea to the next level. After all, she was Sabine-fucking-Cowan. She hadn't just built a career — she'd built an empire. If he let her, she'd help him become Trent-fucking-Brooks and together they'd take over the world. She giggled... *Okay, a little bit of an overreach there.* But she couldn't help but smile as she made her way into the elevator with her bulky custodian cart. They made a great team, she and Trent, and he was just the spark she needed to ignite her soul.

Damn, she was falling for him...and that, surprisingly, made her smile more, even if her heart was thundering with panic. *Let them in and they'll shred you to bits...* But somehow, Trent had slipped past her defenses and now she just couldn't imagine herself without him. Even if her head was telling her one thing, she wasn't feeling it that way. He'd let his constraints go tonight, let her unleash a side of him that he'd probably never shown anyone before. And that was not a gift she'd squander. It might have started as a fun little fling, but somewhere along the line, Sabine had deepened it and now she was committed and craving more.

Chapter Seven

He couldn't be pissed off at Sabine for her little game. The tease had been intense, and even if she had lashed his dick to the point of bruising, it was a good kind of pain. He felt unleashed and excited for what would come next. Not only did he feel like a new man, but she'd left him some ideas on his computer that had helped him nail the improved proposal direction for Franklin Spec. It had been so inspirational that he'd pushed through and worked the creative team hard, getting the storyboards to Franklin Spec by the next afternoon. Everyone had been impressed, including himself. And he was still riding high from it all. If he could pound on his chest and bellow his success without looking like a crazy person, he would. But he tucked that excitement back where it belonged.

"Well done, son." Roy was in his office days later, sitting in the chair Trent had fucked Sabine on twice.

Trent was struggling to keep his grin under control, flashes of Sabine's glistening pussy were rolling through his brain and making his dick hard all over again.

"It was a stroke of inspiration I can't quite explain, but it worked." This time he let the smile tweak his lips. Roy would take it as pride, even though Trent was laughing to himself about whether or not there was cum all over the carpet under Roy's feet.

"The partners are happy," Roy said.

Trent sobered at that statement, giving a silent '*thank fuck*' for that. He'd wanted to make a name for himself. Having come from a small town where it was assumed a person would follow in their father's footsteps, Trent had always wanted more. He could have gone the lawyer route. Harvard, after all, was the breeding ground of many a successful attorney, but instead, he'd fallen hard for marketing and sales, venturing into a business degree where he'd excelled.

When Roy had come calling, stating he'd been following Trent's building presence in the school's advertising world, Trent had been stunned and honored. Working for a giant like Morgan and Miller would prove to everyone that he was capable of much more than being a small-town butcher. The quiet life had never suited him. He'd always craved the excitement of the big city. Coming to work for Roy in New York had been a dream come true — and one that he'd only just started to explore. He wasn't ready to give up on his dream or lose it over a scandal that he hadn't orchestrated. So, yeah, he was glad that the partners had forgiven him.

Ellie brought a coffee in for Roy. "Thanks, hon."

Trent waved her a 'no thanks' when she motioned that she'd get something for him.

She gave him a quick thumbs-up as she walked out, closing the door behind her, a big smile on her lips. Everyone was feeling the afterglow of their success.

"Franklin Spec signed all the agreements this morning. This partnership will bring a lot of good exposure to M&M. You did great work and saved a potential disaster."

Trent leaned back in his chair, feeling a little smug. The praise was nice and he knew deserved it. "I didn't work alone. Ellie and the team really pulled off a miracle." *And Sabine...* She'd really given him what he'd needed...in more ways than one.

Roy waved away the comment. "Everyone will be compensated come bonus time. Don't you worry about that."

Trent would have to compensate Sabine. His mind drifted to her lush body and all the ways he could give her a bonus. His dick tented his pants, throbbing, as usual, for release. He coughed, moved his chair closer to his desk and tried to ignore it.

"More importantly," Roy continued, snapping Trent from his lusty thoughts, "it's helping to clear all that nasty business regarding Sabine from the minds of everyone. Although her filth is ever present in the city. Her sex clubs..." He spat the words. "A deplorable business practice—what she's done to her father's company." He shook his head. "Well, I'm just glad you've followed my advice and rid yourself of her toxic influence. She would have brought you down to rock bottom in no time. I've seen it happen before. Other young men—"

A flash of jealousy struck Trent right in the gut. "Sir." Trent cleared his throat again and sat up straighter, adjusting his tie in the process. "If you don't mind, I'd rather not discuss that woman anymore. If we could just focus on more positive things…"

Bashing Sabine seemed to be one of Roy's favorite things and Roy could be brutal with his accusations. This was a new one, though, that other men had fallen in with Sabine and had been destroyed. Trent found it hard to swallow—or maybe he just didn't want to go down that road in his mind. The thought of her touching another man made him growl.

"Well, she almost got you with those photos. That's all I'm saying." Roy sipped his coffee. "It's a good thing you took my advice. Others haven't been so fortunate."

Trent's thoughts flicked to the leaked photos and the video that had almost destroyed his career. Was it possible that she had released those? Did she get a kick out of torturing men? Okay, yes, she did. He knew that first-hand. But was she maliciously motivated? They'd never actually talked about the leak. He'd been focused on the excitement of their relationship, and really, he didn't want to know. The truth could be a huge buzzkill.

Besides, she'd helped him massively the other night, not only by fucking his stress away, which was just what he'd needed, but also by helping him nail a killer proposal with her ingenious suggestions. That experience, of Sabine helping him, doing something that showed she cared, didn't fit with Roy's interpretation of her. She was not cold-hearted or seemingly out to get him.

Roy nodded then pushed himself up from the chair. "I've got a meeting to get to. I just wanted to come by and congratulate you. Good work, son. You've proven yourself once again. Things should be smoother sailing now that you've got your priorities sorted."

So patronizing. "Thank you, sir." Trent bit back what he really wanted to say and shifted in his chair, itching to grab his phone to text Sabine, his thoughts shifting to do exactly what Roy would not want him to do.

He wasn't going to lie. He missed her. And he knew that meant that she was becoming more meaningful to him than just an amazing fuck. Friends with benefits, sure, but there was nothing casual about how he felt toward her.

She'd been away for only a couple of days on business, but he had a sudden possessive need to check in and make sure they still had plans for that night. He wanted to see her, touch her, talk to her. He had his phone in his hand, swiping to check for texts and disappointed when there was nothing from Sabine. She hadn't checked in at all in the time she'd been gone.

"Have a good day, Mr. Miller." Ellie was at the door just as Roy was walking out. "Trent, there's a call from—"

"Not right now, Ellie," Trent said curtly, then winced when both Roy and Ellie looked at him with shock. "Sorry...headache." He lifted his hand to his temple.

He was dwelling suddenly on Sabine's lack of contact. *No messages from her in two days.* She was coming home today, sure, but his phone had been eerily silent.

"Oh, dear. Well, let me get you some medication." Ellie started toward her desk.

"No, thank you, Ellie, I'm fine. I just need a few minutes."

Roy was still frowning. "Take care of yourself, Trent." He waved his hand around. "You've been working straight through on this Franklin business.

Why don't you take the rest of the afternoon off? Go home and get some rest."

"Thank you, sir. I may just do that."

Roy nodded then walked out, saying something to Ellie as he left. She poked her head in and gave him a soft smile before shutting the door.

He checked his phone again, opening his mail to see if she'd messaged him that way. *Nothing.* She'd warned him she'd likely be out of contact for forty-eight hours. That hadn't bothered him until now.

I expect to see you tonight, he texted. *I'll meet you at the airport.*

He stared at his phone, waiting for some indication that she'd gotten it. He'd been thinking on and off about how to repay Sabine for her little game the other night. He wanted to surprise her with something that he knew would excite her and yet also push her boundaries, just as she'd done with him.

Her delayed response to his text gave him another slap of doubt. Maybe she was distracted by someone else. Maybe that was her thing — a string of men all over the country. She'd never agreed to exclusivity with him. There had never been any talk of a monogamous relationship. She was free to do as she wished, he knew that. But he wanted her all to himself. He wanted her to choose him above someone else, so he had to prove to her that he could crank her up and make her crave only him.

But that would only work if she was still interested in him.

He put the phone down, giving himself a mental shake. *What's with all the paranoia?* He had no reason to think she wasn't still into him. Self-doubt wasn't something he was familiar with, at least not as an adult.

The feeling reminded him of being an insecure, acne-riddled teenager, so sure that he'd never get the smell of meat off his hands from working long hours at the family butcher shop. The girls in his small town had called him 'Trent the Terror' for years because of his job and also because, on Halloween, he used to wear his bloody work apron to give out candy. That probably hadn't been the wisest move for his dating life. Girls remembered shit like that.

So yeah, manufacturing rejection from Sabine was putting him right back in awkward teenager territory.

His phone binged. He quickly glanced at the screen.

Pick me up at ten. Gate sixteen.

He let out a long breath of relief. Then she added something else.

Missed you, baby.

And that made him smile. Yeah, okay, she was still into him. He answered her.

Missed you, too.

He decided to move on the plan he had for her. It was a bold idea and one he thought she'd like…up to a point. Then she'd have a decision to make. It would take a bit of setup, but now that he was taking the rest of the day off, that wouldn't be a problem.

She'd wanted him to be aggressive. Dominant. She'd told him that a few times over the weeks they'd been getting to know one another. She'd told him that he had it in him and she'd pushed him to the point of exploding when she'd tied him up and teased him the other night. He'd felt the aggression boiling up, a need to claim her. So he understood now what she'd been talking about. She wanted him to let it all go, no restraints.

She was a take-charge kind of woman. She liked to be dominant in her business life and she was comfortable taking control when they fucked. But she also wanted him to step up and flip the roles every once in a while. She wanted him to surprise her. And he knew surprising her was going to keep her interested in him, because she'd let it slip that so few men surprised her these days.

He'd told her he couldn't see himself saying nasty things to her like she wanted. He'd told her that he believed aggression was too close to rage, and he didn't want to bring anger into their relationship. *What a loser, right?* He could kick himself for that comment and his cheeks heated a bit at the memory. She'd just chuckled indulgently at the time.

When she'd stopped him from reaching orgasm, when she'd kept him from release, he'd seen a shade of red that hadn't been about anger. It had been about taking what was his. And he'd exploded. Now he understood what she needed from him. He'd called her a filthy, dirty tease, words that just popped into his head and out of his mouth, born of frustration. Then he'd chased her down and fucked her hard and fast until they were both screaming with release. It had been liberating, like he didn't have to hold himself back, not that he'd realized he was.

But holding back had kind of been his thing for as long as he could remember, being a gentleman just as his parents had taught him to be. Polite. Accommodating.

That was how a person got what they wanted in the world. But for Trent, it was becoming like a prison—restraining him at work and also, apparently, in his sex life.

Sabine had broken him free. She'd let him lose himself to what had already been there all along. And he liked it…a lot. He was eager to experiment more.

He'd told her that he'd pay her back for the torture and that was what he planned to do—to tease her until she begged him for release, then tease her some more, just because he could.

"Ellie, I'm going to head out for the day." He shut his office door behind him. "And I won't be in tomorrow."

That was a split-second decision that just felt right. He'd been working his ass off for months without a break. If he was going to take charge of his sex life, he was going to take charge of other areas of his life too. After the Franklin situation, Trent had come to realize that Roy needed him more than he needed Roy. He valued working at Morgan and Miller but that didn't mean he'd continue to take shit over elements of his personal life that Roy disapproved of.

He was owed some time off, and after tonight, if things went according to plan, Trent had a feeling that he would truly embrace the more dominant side of himself. So, if Roy had the urge to comment on his personal life again, Trent would have a thing or two to say back.

Chapter Eight

He was wearing jeans and a button-up shirt, more casual than his usual work attire. His hair looked to be recently washed, his curls still damp. He'd shaved as well. Everything about him was fresh, like he'd had hours to relax before she'd arrived. It wasn't the norm, considering he was usually run ragged by Roy and his cronies, treating Trent like he was some kind of lapdog when they knew, just as well as she did, that he was the star that had saved their entire fucking corporation with his ingenious ad campaigns. He brought a youthful expertise to the company and they were treating him like a servant.

It wasn't the first time Roy had sucked the life out of someone.

But never mind that. It was not the time to dwell in the past. Now was all about Trent. He looked refreshed and happy to see her, his dimples popping with his bright smile, a welcome sight for her. She had missed him terribly while she'd been gone—more than she maybe wanted to admit to herself.

He'd brought her flowers, which was sweet. Tiger lilies, which she loved, and a chauffeured car, not her usual service.

"You didn't have to go to the expense. I could have called Adam to arrange something."

He swept her up in his arms, right there on the sidewalk for all to see, and kissed her deeply, delving his tongue into her mouth, devouring her with such ferocity that she realized he'd really missed her too.

She was dizzy when he pulled away. "Oh…" She felt an uncharacteristic heat on her cheeks as she glanced around to see if any paparazzi were about. But they were standing in the semi-dark, maybe too dark for anyone to notice who she was. It had happened before. Her private jet occasionally landed at this less-used terminal and the photographers typically didn't bother with her here. But there was no way Trent would have known it. So, that meant he was taking some risks for her. *Interesting and intriguing.* She wondered what had changed. Was he finally taking charge of his life and no longer worrying about the judgment of Morgan and Miller?

That was a conversation for later, because if he was ready to move on, career-wise, she had some ideas.

"Let's go." He took her hand and pulled her into the car with him, helping her move her big purse to the floor so she could climb in.

The opaque glass was up, separating them from the driver. Even so, as soon as her door shut, they were moving. Trent hadn't needed to say a word.

"Where are we headed?" She accepted a glass of champagne.

"It's a surprise." With a smirk he held up a pretty black satin strip of cloth. "May I?" He motioned to her face.

She nearly choked on her drink. "Um…okay." She smiled. It really would be a surprise. She turned slightly so that he could put the soft cloth over her eyes, tying it snugly so that she couldn't see any light. She had to admit, though, that it was slightly disorienting and more than a little exciting.

"No peeking," he said softly, his lips very close to her ear.

It sent a shiver over her skin. She bit her bottom lip and shook her head. "Wouldn't dream of it."

She guided her drink to her lips, not exactly an easy thing when she couldn't see what she was doing, but she managed without spilling anything down her front.

"Can I feed you?"

She'd already caught the scent of food—something delicious, heavy on the garlic, which she loved.

"Yes, please. I'm starving." She licked her lips and inched herself toward where she thought he was. The car was big, but not too big. She could feel the heat from his body to her right, close enough that his arm brushed hers.

He brought something warm to her lips and she opened obediently.

"Mm-m-m," she moaned, savoring the buttery, garlic-coated mussel.

"It's an aphrodisiac, isn't it?" Trent said as he pressed a second one to her lips.

"So I've heard." She giggled as she swallowed the next offering. "But I don't really need anything like that to get me cranked up." *I just need you.* She bit back that confession, though, and swallowed another mussel.

Maybe she didn't *need* him, per se, but she wanted Trent pressed on top of her, the weight of him making it hard to breathe as he rolled his hips and fucked her properly. There was something to be said for monogamy. Going for a couple of days without a sexual partner did make her long more for sex. But it wasn't just that, she knew, because she hadn't wanted to be with anyone but Trent since she'd met him. Being apart from him had made her desperate for his touch in a way that made her think she was addicted to the man.

"Mm-m-m." She moaned, as much for the mussel as the thought of him slipping his cock deep inside of her, pumping her until she screamed.

"I'm going to undress you," he said.

"Yes, please!" She straightened her back, turning toward him so he could unbutton her blouse.

He brushed his fingers against her tit as he did, making her throb harder for his touch. "Because I need to disguise you."

"Oh yeah?" She felt another shiver. This was getting exciting. "Are you taking me somewhere public?"

"Yes, I am. But no one will know who you are — not unless you wish it."

Well, I won't wish it, sweetheart. But again, she kept that to herself. She didn't want to undermine his little game or make it seem like he wasn't in control, which she knew this was all about. But there was no way she was going to expose herself and put Trent at risk of discovery. If the media caught wind of them together again, he'd lose everything at M&M. She knew how ruthless they could be, but if Trent had his heart set on working there, she wasn't going to do anything that would fuck it up.

"You have my consent, Trent, to undress me, to touch me, to fuck me, to tease me, whatever… I consent." She leaned toward him, guessing at where his lips were, hers puckered.

He chuckled, but instead of kissing her, he gripped her jaw tightly, stopping her from moving forward. "Sit back," he ordered, "arms behind your head, linked together. Don't move them until I tell you to."

With eyes wide behind the blindfold, Sabine snapped to attention, doing exactly as he'd asked, his change of tone so surprising that her pussy clenched with desire.

He slowly unbuttoned her blouse all the way and pulled it off her arms, one by one, moving her, nudging her fingers to allow him to slip the fabric off. She kept her arms in place, only moving to accommodate him as he stripped her bare — first her blouse then her skirt.

"Spread your knees."

She wasn't wearing panties, of course, so spreading herself meant she was on display, the air against her pussy making her wetter.

He gripped her breasts, cupping them through her bra before he pulled the cups back enough so that her nipples popped free. He rubbed his thumbs over them, pushing down hard so that they abraded against the edge of her bra then flicked up again.

"You have the most beautiful tits." His tone was reverent. "I want to see you come just from sucking them, like you promised."

He unclasped her bra and pushed the cups off her breasts.

"You said chocolate sauce, but I prefer butterscotch."

She licked her lips and nodded. "I like butterscotch."

"I like butterscotch, *Sir*," he corrected.

Sabine squirmed with delight. "Yes, Sir. I like butterscotch, Sir."

He grunted his approval then busied himself with opening and clanging things. When he returned to her, he pressed something against her lips.

Strawberry dipped in butterscotch. Delicious.

As she was chewing, he slipped his fingers into her pussy, making her moan around the food. He used his thumb to rub her clit.

"You're very wet, Sabine," he said, his voice guttural. "Have you been thinking of me today?"

She gulped, nodded. "Yes, Sir."

"Good girl," he said.

Something warm touched her nipple—a brush of warmth, actually. Circling, coating, the butterscotch sauce was almost too warm to tolerate, first on one breast then the other. He removed his fingers from her pussy and pressed them to her lips.

She opened her mouth wide, letting him coat her tongue in her own juices as he leaned in and took one of her nipples into his mouth, sucking hard, scraping his teeth down to lick away the butterscotch before pulling back.

"Mm-m-m, delicious."

She sucked in a breath, biting her own lip in response.

He licked along her lips, pushing butterscotch into her mouth, tangling his tongue with hers. The kiss was deep and messy. Saliva and butterscotch dripped down her chin. Her body was revving higher and higher. It might be possible for her to come just from a kiss. That was how cranked up she was.

But he pulled back from her lips and left a trail of soft kisses down her neck until he got to her tits. He slurped and sucked away at one nipple while he flicked and teased the other with his fingers.

He moved back and forth, pinching and licking, rolling and rubbing, murmuring against her flesh. "You're so fucking hot, Sabine." He sucked her breast into his mouth, as much as he could, and twirled his tongue over her nipple. Her body coiled, twisting up so tight that she was just about to blow.

Then he stopped.

And she wanted to scream.

But he chuckled. "Payback's a bitch, eh?"

He smacked her tits, one then the other. "You'll come when I say you can come. Right, Sabine?"

Her mouth dropped open but she nodded eagerly.

"Yes, *Sir*," he reminded with another slap to her tits.

"Yes, Sir," she repeated.

"Good girl," he said. He paused. "I want to fuck your tits. Lie down."

He helped her slip lower then positioned her hands on either side of her breasts, pushing them together so that they made a nice cushion for him.

"I want to see," she said.

He responded with another firm smack on her tit. "No."

He dripped something hot along her breasts, coating the crease she'd made between them. She could hear as he unzipped his pants and grunted as he positioned himself over her—not too easy in the limo, but he managed. His cock slipped between her tits, pushing them apart so she had to apply more pressure with her hands to keep them together. As he fucked her, he was playing with her nipples, rolling them between his fingers, somehow balancing himself, hitting her chin with his cock as he thrust hard but slowly over and over. She wiggled her ass, her pussy aching. She so badly wanted to stroke her clit, to lift her blindfold and watch him, but instead, she had to rely on the feel of it, the sensation of his dick moving in and out, the groans that rumbled through him then the hot spurt of his cum hitting her face.

She licked her lips, tasting the salty tang of him, mixed with butterscotch.

He moved down her body, spreading her legs once again, and nestled there. She nearly bucked right off the seat as he penetrated her with his tongue. He made long, deep licks from her asshole to her pussy, slurping up her cream and nipping at her clit before sucking hard there too.

She was so ramped up that she felt the buzz of her orgasm rising again.

"Trent, I need this…" Then she bit her lip, hard.

He chuckled. "I know you do, baby," he said. Then he pulled away from her completely.

Without thinking she moved her hand down as if to stroke herself. He *tsked* at her, grabbing her hands, capturing both her wrists.

"Naughty girl, I didn't say you could do that." He wrapped something around her wrists, binding them tightly before yanking them up high until they were suspended above her head.

He slapped the side of her breast again, leaving a sting that burned her skin. She squirmed beneath him.

"I've got just the punishment for you." He ran something cold and hard against her hip. "I'm going to slip these inside your pussy and you're going to keep them there or you'll be punished."

Ben Wa balls. She'd experienced them before, and depending on the size, they were not too difficult to keep in place. These felt a little on the large side, though, so she'd have to concentrate. She had tight muscles and she was up for the challenge, but all the same, there was a tantalizing impulse to disobey.

He opened her pussy lips, using his fingers to delve into her, rubbing her clit briefly and eliciting a moan of frustration as he pulled her from her thoughts.

"It's the least I can do, considering how you tortured me." He chuckled.

He pushed the balls into her and she gripped them tight with her pussy. The trick would be keeping them from slipping out when she had to walk. With how wet she was, the damn things could just slide right out with the first step she took.

"We're almost there. I'm going to clean you up and get you dressed."

He used a warm cloth to wipe her face and her breasts, spending some extra time circling her nipples and alternating between rough and soft, making her throb even more intensely than he already had.

Had he been studying while she'd been gone? Everything he was doing was cranking her up to unbearable levels. The teasing, the commands, the possession of her body — all of it was a total turn-on.

"Sit up," he ordered and helped her maneuver, her arms still above her head.

He draped a soft cloth over her shoulders. If felt like a cloak. It was long and billowing with a clasp that he secured at her collarbone, brushing his fingers between her breasts when he'd finished latching it closed.

"You will not speak. You will walk behind me and I will guide you. You will keep the hood over your head and you will do exactly as I say. Is that understood?"

Sabine gulped and nodded. "Yes, Sir."

"And if those balls drop, you're going to regret it. I have ways to keep you from climaxing too, sweetie."

She moaned her response to that, delighted by Trent's mastery of power and control. This was exactly what she'd been craving. She clenched her knees tight, scared that her slick pussy would expel the balls just because the threat of punishment was too tempting.

"One more thing," he said, his tone dark.

She felt him shift away from her, heard the clicking of metal then felt the press of it against her nipples.

"You said you liked some pain."

She winced, sucking her lip from crying out as he clamped her nipples, the bite of the metal teeth intense against her throbbing flesh.

"Oh-h, baby, does that hurt?" He leaned toward her, licking the tips of her nipples, clamps and all, and rubbing her clit at the same time.

She writhed against him, the torment of his attention making her pant. "Trent," she breathed.

"You begging, sweetie?" Trent gave her one last lick then pulled away.

The clamps made her nipples burn. As long as he didn't touch her, she'd be fine. She so wanted him to touch her, though.

"We're here," he said as he released her arms from their suspension but not their binding. "Remember what I said. Keep those balls inside you."

The cloth of her cloak pressed against her aching nipples and she sucked in a breath that sounded like a moan.

"Be quiet," he ordered.

She clamped her lips shut and nodded. He raised her hood to fall over her head and face. No one would know who was under the cloak and it was too big for someone to peek in. She smiled to herself, trembling a bit. He was protecting her, keeping her identity a secret, which she was grateful for because, really, as much as she liked playing the role of a submissive, there was no way she wanted the world to know that Sabine Cowan, mistress bitch of smut, was bowing to any man.

Chapter Nine

He led her inside the club. Her club, actually, and one he knew she didn't frequent often. He'd done his research. It wasn't too hard to figure out that while the staff was on alert, expecting her to pop by for a spot check on any given day, she hadn't been by in some time. Maybe that was because it was in New Jersey, a little off the beaten path. Or maybe it was because it had what the deep web called a Fuck Room. As soon as Trent had stumbled onto it, he knew it was exactly what he'd been looking for — a way to test Sabine's boundaries.

A part of him half-expected that she'd recognize the sounds, that she would tune in to the music being played or the sweet, cloying smell that wafted all around them. But she didn't seem to register where they were in any way he could tell — not that it was easy to tell with her under a huge cloak. She crossed the threshold and followed obediently, without any sign of hesitation.

He'd made prior arrangements. The staff knew not to speak to his *slave* and he'd paid a lot for their discretion. He suspected that he'd been vetted by her security team in some way but had hoped that was where the information had stopped, not reaching Sabine to ruin the surprise. They knew who he was, and they knew who he'd likely be bringing to entertain there.

Once inside, they were guided to the back and down a flight of stairs. He helped Sabine navigate but otherwise didn't acknowledge her. The ribbon he'd used to bind her wrists had a length on it like a leash, so he was able to guide her closely without having to touch her.

He'd watched porn after porn in the days that she'd been gone, masturbating furiously at all the sexy ideas they offered. Sabine wanted aggression from him. She wanted to take on the role of a sub. None of it felt foreign to him, despite the fact that he'd never ventured into that kind of territory before now. He was enjoying it immensely. And he could tell she was too. Her pussy had been so slick in the car that the thought of it made his dick jolt almost painfully. He'd fucked her tits, but what he really wanted was to sink into her juicy cunt and fuck her properly. But there'd be time for that.

"Your room, Mr. Brooks… Everything is exactly as you requested," the pretty, dark-haired escort said as she handed him the key with a nod of understanding that she needn't say anything more.

He moved Sabine inside and shut the door behind them, turning the key in the lock. No one would come in to disturb them unless he desired them to. There would be no surprises either. Not for him, anyway.

He moved Sabine to the center of the room, where there was a low-hanging hook. He lifted her arms and latched the ribbon to it, hoisting her almost to her tiptoes. She gasped under the hood but otherwise didn't speak.

He walked to the table that was against the wall. All the tools he'd asked for were there.

"Are those balls still in you?" he called over his shoulder.

"Yes, Sir," she answered.

He smiled. *Yes, Sir.* He liked those words out of her pretty little mouth. Maybe he'd get her to say them again with his cock between her lips, drooling on his dick as she tried to speak. His grin widened.

He picked up a leather-corded flogger. It had a sturdy braided handle with slim, stiff little tails that would leave a nice mark on her flesh. He ran it over his hand, smacking against his palm. The sound it made caused her to rustle on her hook, the movement of the cloth and the rattling of the chain making him smile. "Be right there, sweetheart."

He turned back to the table and picked up the small finger vibrator. It buzzed to life with a press of his thumb. *Perfect.* He slipped it onto his index finger and turned toward Sabine. Her legs were crossed at the ankles, her thighs pressed together tightly, and she was swaying slightly on the hook.

"You having a hard time there, Sabine?"

She squeezed her legs tighter in response, whimpering a little when he turned the vibrator on.

"I'll tell you what," he said as he unclasped the cloak and let it fall to the floor, pooling at the tips of her toes. "If you can keep them in through an orgasm, I'll reward you with my cock. If you can't, I'm going to punish you severely."

She nodded eagerly, her smile saying she expected to win that challenge.

He ran the tip of the flogger's handle over her breast, circling her nipple and eliciting a moan from between her clenched lips. The nipple clamps were making her skin turn a vibrant red. He knew, from experimenting on himself, that those fuckers were tight as hell. He also knew that as soon as he released her nipples, she'd have a flood of relief so great that she'd probably come on the spot. He circled one more time with the flogger before continuing down to her pussy and using the handle to rub against the top of her clit hood, shifting her piercing up and down in the process. She undulated her hips, moving into the handle, biting her bottom lip and looking delicious in her agony.

He pulled the handle away and replaced it with the tiny vibrator on his finger. The second it touched her skin she jolted, arching her back and releasing a long moan from her lips. He unclasped one of the nipple clamps then immediately latched on to her with his lips, sucking hard, flicking harder, and in that action alone, she exploded. Her orgasm rippled through her, making her cry out, rocking her hips as she pressed herself harder against the vibrator. He let her ride it out, knowing that each second that passed was torture, her concentration split between enjoying the orgasm and keeping those balls in place.

He chuckled against her tit, sucking one more time before pulling away. Her whole breast was red now, not just the tip. "Well, well, well, you managed to keep them in." He leaned into her, lips pressed to her ear. "I'm still going to punish you."

She whimpered. He liked that sound. Pulling way, he smacked her tits a few times with the flogger, making sure it left red marks but didn't break her skin. She squirmed away from him with each successive hit but always swung back for the next.

"You want me to spank you, Sabine?" He cupped one breast, the one without the clamp, palming away the sting those tails had no doubt caused.

She moaned. "Yes, Sir."

"Because you're a dirty girl, aren't you?" He squeezed her nipple.

She gasped, crying out a little. "Yes, very dirty."

"That's what I thought."

He went back to the table and grabbed the larger of the paddles there. He could use his hand, and maybe he would later, but right now he wanted to feel what it was like to paddle her bare ass.

"I forbid you from coming," he ordered.

She moaned in response.

He sucked hard on her free nipple, teasing the clamped one with his fingers until she was writhing again. He unclasped the remaining clamp, flicking slowly as her nipple certainly throbbed and burned for him. "Do not come, Sabine."

She twisted and groaned, her legs squeezed closed, and somehow she managed to keep herself from exploding.

"Spread your legs a shoulder-width apart." He reached up and adjusted the hook a bit, lowering it enough so that she could get a good bearing. "Arch your back and bend over a little." He moved behind her, palming her ass as he did.

The second her feet fell flat to the floor, she did what he'd ordered, her pretty, plump ass on display, her tits swaying as she angled herself so that he could properly spank her.

He lifted the paddle then hesitated. This was hot, so fucking hot that he'd gotten caught up in it all. But he'd never paddled a woman before. Sure, he'd watched videos and he could develop technique, but he didn't really want to hurt her.

"Sabine," he said, "do you want this?"

"Yes, I do…" she said breathlessly. "I do, Sir."

He smiled, feeling reassured. They'd discussed safewords. Hers was 'teddy' as in 'bear'. His was 'ketchup'…as in 'hot dog'. It had made her laugh at the time.

He wiped the smile from his face. It was time to get down to it. "No squirming."

"Yes, Sir."

"You'll take every spank and you'll thank me for it."

"Yes, Sir."

He put his hand on her ass, rubbing along the smooth curve of her skin. He loved her ass. There was ample cushion he could sink into…but not yet. He pulled his arm back then brought the paddle down. *Smack!*

"Thank you," she cried out.

Smack!

"T-t-thank y-y-you."

Smack!

Smack!

Smack!

She squeezed her legs together, rocking her hips. *Fuck me! She's having an orgasm.*

Trent threw the paddle down, ripped his pants open and pulled her hips up. He hooked his finger into the loop attached to the balls and yanked them out before pounding his cock deep inside her.

They both cried out. Her pussy milked him, gripping tight as she spasmed, her body shaking with the intensity of it.

He fucked her through her climax and kept going even as she slumped, her limbs like noodles. With his hands on her hips, he pumped her hard, his balls ready to burst. She arched back into him, giving him more access, locking her legs once again. He reached around and cupped her swaying tits, squeezing them both before teasing her nipples, the hard little buds hot to the touch.

Her moan was one long sound, matching the feeling that ripped through his body as he finally released his cum deep inside her.

"Fuck me!" he bellowed and continued to thrust, pulling on her nipples then cupping her tits.

He slowed as the last ripples of pleasure coursed through him. He slumped his body over her back, still holding her breasts.

"You know what I've been thinking about all day?" he asked.

"What?" She panted.

Her body was slicked with sweat. He licked her shoulder. "I've been thinking about sticking a dildo in your pussy while I fuck your asshole."

She moaned.

He bit her skin. "You want me to do that, dirty girl?"

She nodded. "Yes, Sir."

He pulled his cock out of her, mourning the loss of her heat. But it wouldn't be for long.

Moving back to the table, he grabbed one of the dildos and the bottle of lube. When he turned back to face her, he had to stop and take her in. She was hanging there, looking so pretty. The blindfold was a little lopsided — still covering her eyes, but just barely. Her arms were straining, her tits swaying, her feet shoulder-width apart, planted firmly. She looked vulnerable and yet still very powerful. *This woman...* She was everything he could ever wish for.

He smiled as he approached, moving behind her once again. Cum was dripping from her pussy to the floor. His cum. He liked that she let him fuck her unprotected. They both preferred it. They'd gotten tested once they'd decided to keep fucking, with the expectation that if they had sex with anyone else, they'd use protection. But he wasn't going to be fucking anyone else. He didn't want to. It was Sabine he craved above all others.

That niggling jolt of jealousy returned. What if she had been fucking someone else while she had been traveling? What if Roy was right and she like to fuck around with young men?

He pushed that thought away again. Jealousy was not attractive, he knew that, and there was no place for it here.

"Did you miss me?" he asked, moving behind her once again.

"Yes," she breathed.

"How much?" She'd shifted her legs closed a bit so he nudged her feet apart again with his leg. She complied, legs shoulder width apart, ass in the air.

"You're the only person on my mind" — she gulped — "always."

He smiled, his chest heating with triumph. "You think about me a lot?"

She gasped as he squirted lube into her ass crack then rubbed it into her hole, fingering her to get her all slicked up.

"I can't stop thinking about you, Trent." And the way she said it, he knew she wasn't lying. He knew she felt the same way about him as he did about her.

"Me too, Sabine." He lubed up the dildo. "You're the only one I think about."

He let the bottle hit the floor then moved into Sabine, his cock nudging her ass as he reached around and slid the dildo up and down her pussy lips.

"I'm going to stick my fat cock into your ass."

"Uh-huh," she said breathlessly.

"And I'm going to fuck you with this dildo."

"Yes, please." Her voice was gruff, full of lust. "You know I love double penetration."

He slipped the dildo deep inside her pussy, pumping her a few times. Yeah, she'd told him. Her fantasy was two guys at once, something he really didn't think he'd ever be up for. But he could do this with her, fill her up with a hard, thick dildo and his cock.

"Do you know where we are?" he grunted against her as he slid his cock up and down her ass crack.

"No," she gasped out.

He reached up and untied her blindfold. "Do you recognize this place?"

She turned her head a few times — blinking, taking in the room — then she gasped again. "Yes."

"Do you know what we can do in this room?"

He reached over and tapped next to the big red button that was on the wall.

"Yes." Her voice quivered.

He positioned his cock against her asshole. "Do you want me to push this button?"

He bit his lip, waiting for her response. This was it. Would she be willing to cross a boundary with him?

His finger was poised on the button. He brought her around, shifting her body so she could see it.

"I-I…" Her whole body shook.

She was going to say no. This was going too far. *Stupid idea.* One push of the button and two panels on each wall would drop, exposing them to voyeurs — customers who came in to watch people fuck. They could make demands too. Offer suggestions to perhaps get exactly what they wanted. It was risky. They would recognize Sabine for sure.

He started to lower his hand, feeling like shit. It was too much. Why would he ask her to do something like this when he wasn't exactly willing to cross all his boundaries?

"Yes, Sir." Her voice was a whisper.

Huh?

She cleared her throat. "Yes, Sir," she said more clearly.

"You want me to push this button?"

She gulped and nodded. "Yes. Do it."

She pushed her hips back, lifting her ass to his cock.

His brain exploded. *She said yes!* She trusted him so much to do that with him. His heart felt so full in that moment, like she'd given him the best gift imaginable.

He pushed the button and, as the panels started to move, he shoved his dick deep into her ass and they both cried out.

Fuck, I love this woman.

Chapter Ten

She had a confession to make... Trent's little experiment in dominance turned her on more than she wanted him to know — even his idea to expose her to a crowd. At first she'd screamed 'no' in her head, once she'd realized where they were, but then she remembered something really important about the New Jersey location. It had notoriously low attendance. Phones were turned in at the door and security was as vigilant as possible, because, well, the Fuck Room was highly illegal. The clients who knew about it paid good money to be there, but it was an exclusive club, not for the general public. While there were likely people on the other side of the one-way mirrors, they would only be able to talk about what happened, and most valued their own privacy so much that they never would.

That didn't mean there wasn't any risk — or that she hadn't taken a big step for Trent. What they'd done had pushed her boundaries in a big way. Being vulnerable and exposed as a sub was not something Sabine had thought she'd want anyone to know about. But the thrill was absolutely worth it. And knowing that she was taking that step with Trent, without him putting his own job at risk due to the lessened possibility of exposure, was worth it too. She'd tell him, of course, just so that they didn't have secrets from one another. But she wanted to be delicate about that. He was just starting to experiment with his own thresholds. She didn't want to discourage him from exploring those limits by confessing that there really wasn't much of a potential problem at all.

The reality was that Adam had known the second Trent had started to roll out his plan. He'd texted her to let her know that Trent had something in the works, just not what it was, leaving it up to her to decide if she wanted the surprise or not. She had told Adam to let it be. Whatever Trent had planned, she could handle. And yes, she trusted him. She was glad she'd let his idea play out the way it had. The night before had been unbelievable for so many reasons. Trent had exceeded all her expectations. She was hooked, craving more, and she didn't even regret that feeling, despite the fact that it made her vulnerable. She cared about him…wanted to be with him indefinitely. It was an exciting prospect for Sabine to think about a future with Trent—not just because of the sexual stuff but also because he got her. He was kind and understanding and sweet, intelligent and witty…but also wicked. What more could a woman ask for from a partner? *And those dimples? Sheesh!*

Sabine smiled to herself, running her fingers over her lips, feeling the imprint of his kisses. She really did love that he'd taken such a risk for her and for demanding that she push her limits.

All the same, she'd asked Adam to keep his ear to the clubs to see if any rumors were spreading about her using the Fuck Room at a Kitty Boutique. She wasn't worried—not exceedingly so, anyway. And besides, showing a submissive side of herself, while cringe-worthy to her, wasn't exactly bad for business either. Sex did sell, especially if she was endorsing it. She'd enjoyed using the Fuck Room and could think of more ways to experiment there with Trent.

Her body ached from all the use. They'd fucked all night. Trent and his virile body had kept her ramped up and hot until she'd collapsed from exhaustion. He'd carried her out of there in her cloak, protecting her identity in the end, which had been very valiant.

They'd gone back to her condo in the city at her insistence. She liked the idea of having him in her bed, in her private space. She wasn't going to lie. Curling up next to him and sleeping until morning had been the cherry on top of the ice cream sundae. She had never been one for cuddling post-sex, but with Trent and his big body, the way he nuzzled her neck and held her around the waist, one hand cupped to her breast, it was deliciously comforting—and something she could get used to for sure. That was yet another thing she wasn't quite ready to admit out loud.

She'd left him sleeping it off in her room, closing the door to her office so that she could get some work done and not be distracted by the haphazard way he draped his arm over his head or how the sheets pulled taut over his muscles.

She gave her head a shake and sighed. She'd never get anything done at this rate.

"I've got some intel on the Kitty Cat party video leak," Adam said as he walked into her office, two coffees in his hands. He had a key to all her places and could come and go as he pleased.

She met his gaze with wide eyes, vanishing any lusty thoughts of Trent. "What'd you find?" She gratefully accepted the coffee. She wasn't the most domesticated woman around. Making her own coffee was something she could do but didn't always think of doing. Adam knew that. He also knew what kind of jolt she'd need after a night out.

"I've been trying to track down the source and got a lead through Sam Henderson."

Ah yes, Sam — an old friend from her high school days. He wasn't exactly on her side all the time but he did like money — and Sabine had a lot of that. "Did Sam have any ideas on where the video originated from?"

She'd already had Adam look into all the guests, trying to suss out if there was anyone there who would have something to gain by leaking the photo and video from the Kitty Cat party. Opportunism was one thing, but that video and those photos were put out there to tarnish the legitimate side of her business. If it could happen there, even with all of her security measures in place, it could happen anywhere. There were some aspects of what she did that could land her in a lot of trouble. It was nothing that money couldn't buy her way out of, but still, she didn't want to go down that route if it could be avoided.

All the guests that night had turned in their phones. That was standard practice at all her events. And all the guests had also been hand-picked as high flyers, so they had something to lose either by exposure or by her business being negatively impacted. If she had taken a hit, so would they. There would be no more escorts for them, not to mention what they didn't know about…her extensive database containing all manner of secrets. It would be good leverage if it came to that. It had already gotten her out of many sticky situations in the past. At some point, most influential men found their way to one of her services, and she was always ready to collect information when it came to her.

"I'm digging deeper into the servers that were on that night. It took a bit of cash, but Sam did suggest that it was someone on staff."

None of her girls, she was sure. All of her Kitty Cats were vetted extensively. Sabine nodded. "Well, the sooner we find out, the sooner we can blacklist the perpetrator. I don't want a snake on the roll call for events."

It was one thing to go after her, but to potentially risk Trent's budding career too? That was unacceptable. Yes, he'd likely been collateral damage, but still, she had feelings about Trent—strong feelings—and she wanted some justice for him. She'd invited him to that party, so she was responsible for what had happened to him.

"Are you keeping your appointments today?" Adam pulled out his phone and scrolled. "You've got a meeting with Lush Lips at one and Kinkster Rig at three."

Sabine rubbed her head, sighing, a headache building behind her eyes. "I've already rescheduled Kinkster Rig twice. I'll make it to that one. Call Eva at Lush Lips and tell her something came up."

Adam nodded as he started walking away. "You got it, boss." He put the phone to his ear, giving her a thumbs-up gesture then grabbing his coffee as he walked out. He'd keep himself busy until she needed him. He was good like that.

But right now she wanted to crawl back into bed and let Trent take care of her throbbing head. Orgasms worked wonders for that.

She closed her laptop and pushed her chair back. She'd showered and put on a silk robe when she'd gotten up, but that was it. She loved the sensation of silk on her bare flesh — the way it slid, like a feather, so delicate along her sensitive skin. She undid the tie at her waist and let the robe slip off her shoulders. She had some bruises on her breasts and her ab muscles were sore. Her ache for Trent, though, made it all worth it. She wanted to be with him all the time. She hadn't even glanced at another man since she'd started this, whatever it was, with Trent. They hadn't explicitly said they were monogamous, but she was behaving as though they had, which was unusual for her. And, if she were honest, a little frightening.

Unlike most of the relationships she'd had in her life, her interest in Trent hadn't started fizzling out. She was just as intrigued as she had been the first day they'd met. His capacity for change was amazing. She'd unleashed his alpha and now he was unstoppable. Dominant in all the right ways, but he was still invested in her desires and her fantasies. *Too good to be true.*

She sighed again, her headache kicking up a notch, then made her way back to her bedroom.

Trent was sprawled out, sleeping on his back, with scruff on his jaw and his hair tussled in a super-sexy way. He was the epitome of seductive — just the right amount of definition, not too bulky but fit, strong. His dick, which was twitching under the covers, almost like it sensed her presence, was perfect too. It was big, thick and hooked, and she couldn't seem to get enough of it. Every hole he stuffed it in felt like the best thing ever, each time stretching her out, hitting her in just the right ways.

Her body coiled with desire, her headache toning down somewhat. She licked her lips then climbed onto the bed, ready to wake him up the proper way.

She pulled the covers away, slowly, so that the fabric moved across the sensitive skin of his dick. He stirred but didn't wake. She smiled then lowered so she could touch the head of his dick with her closed lips.

His cock got hard, fast, which made her giggle. He still didn't wake up though. She opened her lips, curving around his crown and blowing lightly as she did, gobbing her saliva along his shaft as she made her way down.

That woke him up.

He opened his eyes with a jolt, his body almost coming off the bed. He saw what she was doing then relaxed with a sly smile.

"Now that's a wake-up call."

She winked but didn't stop, taking him past the gate of her throat so that she could move all the way down to his base. He moaned, moving his hand to her hair, while she moved hers to cup his balls. She massaged his soft, heavy and pulsing balls with her fingers and his shaft with her tongue, pressing hard along his dick as she withdrew...but not completely. She pumped him a few times with her mouth, not taking him quite so deep but giving his head a good rub along the roof of her mouth. He bucked his hips, spurting a bit of precum to the back of her throat. He was so hot, with his eyes on her, hooded and lusty, watching her mouth-fuck him, gripping her hair tight enough for her to wince, and with his dick pulsing. Her pussy was soaked, her clit throbbing.

She unlatched herself and swatted his hand away before she straddled him, letting his dick glide into her pussy with one thrust.

"You're so fucking beautiful, Sabine," he groaned, cupping her breasts.

She nodded. "So are you," she said before throwing her head back and riding him with a slow roll. It felt so good...so damn good. It was like his body in her body just fit exactly right, so right that she was already coiling up for an orgasm, waves washing over her as it built.

But he must have sensed it because he pulled her forward, scooping under her ass so he could flip them, his body on top of hers, his dick never leaving her pussy. She hooked her legs around him, loving the press of his weight on top of her. He wrapped her up in his arms, looking at her with such intensity that she didn't dare look away. She was mesmerized, completely locked in, and so was he.

They rocked together, moving slowly but steadily, gasping for breath, moaning through the sensations but never looking away. Until that moment seized him, where his eyes flashed with a predatory glint and his movements started to grow more frenzied, pulling her up hard and pushing her down harder, his cock slamming her over and over again.

"Yes! Yes!" she cried out, her climax right there, cranked up so high that she thought she'd never crest. But she did, just at the same moment he did, their bodies shuddering together, in unison, spilling passion inside and out.

It went on forever and all Sabine could think was that she'd never had it this good before and she couldn't get enough. She was addicted to the man and it felt so damn wonderful.

* * * *

That wasn't fucking. Not this time. Sabine lay nestled in Trent's arms and she had no desire to get up. She was actually contemplating telling Adam that she wouldn't be making any of her appointments that afternoon. She was way too comfortable. As much as she wanted to, she knew she couldn't blow off another appointment. The Kinkster Rig deal would put a whole new line of products in her retail locations, as well as some of the Kitty Boutiques at the cash, impulse buys. They had a good range of toys and lotions and Sabine had offered a lucrative proposal that would benefit both parties. But she'd missed two appointments already and she really couldn't miss a third. She might be the most appealing gig in the smut industry but she wasn't the only one. She did have competition.

"I need to shower," she moaned.

"I'll join you," he said, nudging her with his hip.

She smacked his chest playfully. "You're insatiable!"

He nuzzled her neck. "Yeah, aren't you?"

"With you? Yes," she admitted, then pushed herself up. "But seriously, I should get ready."

Trent stretched his arms up to cradle is head. "Well, I'm off for the day, so I've got nowhere to be."

"Adam can drive you home if you want—or you could stay here." She moved to the end of the bed. "I won't be back until late though."

"Adam's here?" Trent lowered his arms then sat up.

"Yeah, he came in this morning, to update me on a few things." Sabine got up and started to pad toward the bathroom. "If you want to join me in the shower, I've got a spare ten." She winked over her shoulder then paused, frowning. "What's wrong?"

"You have something with him, right?" Trent ran his hand through his hair, his smile gone, replaced with a scowl. "I mean, fuck, I know you and I aren't exclusive, and he's always around."

Sabine smiled then slipped back into bed. "Yeah, we've fucked plenty of times." She wrapped her arms around Trent. "But I'm not fucking him now."

"And that's all this is? Fucking?" He wasn't looking at her, keeping his eyes down, not returning her embrace either.

"No, I don't think it is." She kissed his jaw. "I like you, Trent, more than a lot. I prefer you to anyone else, even Adam."

"You prefer me…"

She scoffed then pulled away. "If I wanted to be with Adam, I would be." She tried to soften her tone, knowing that Trent wasn't some guy she was just going to toss aside and that she wanted him in her life, but all the same, she wasn't one to indulge insecurity like this. "I'm not going to lie to you and say that I haven't ever been with the man, because I have — but not since we got together."

"I'm not possessive," Trent said, his voice sounding uncertain.

"You could have fooled me." Sabine laughed but kissed him again to soften the statement. "I get it. I live a different kind of life. But I'm telling you that I'm not sleeping with anyone else right now and, if that changes, I'll tell you."

Trent shifted his eyes up, his body stiffening more. "You'll tell me?"

"Yeah." She moved back, disengaging her arms and feeling cold all of a sudden.

His eyes flashed with something she couldn't quite place. Frustration? Anger? She frowned and opened her mouth to question him, but she didn't get a chance.

He pulled himself away completely, getting up a second after that.

"Just like you told me about the video?"

"What video?" She rose to her knees.

"The video from your mansion on the night of the party. You haven't even apologized for that."

Sabine screwed up her face. "What are you talking about?" She felt a flash of anger. She got off the bed.

"Okay, fine. I know it wasn't you who filmed it. Maybe it was Adam, but you knew about it, right? You leaked that video."

Sabine jolted. "I did no such thing!"

Trent flinched. "Oh come on, Sabine. Everyone knows you leaked it. It's all the media is talking about. You love that kind of publicity, even at the expense of someone's career. You hate Roy. I get it, but you never did apologize for what you did. How could this be real between us if we have this baggage?"

He looked like he believed his own bullshit, like he was totally in the right to falsely accuse her of this.

How long had he thought it? From the beginning? Such a typical fucking man. Believing the worst of her. Believing that she'd do that to him.

She could have argued. She could have screamed. Instead, she walked to the bathroom, giving herself time to control her reaction, to wipe the pain that was lashing at her from her face. Just as she reached the door, she said over her shoulder, "If that's the way you think of me then you can let yourself out. I expect you to be gone once I've showered."

She closed the door before he could say anything more.

Her heart hurt and her headache was back. *Fuck!* She leaned against the counter, rubbing her temples and trying to keep her emotions from overflowing. There were tears in her eyes, which pissed her off even more. Why had she let herself become vulnerable with him? She'd actually thought… Well, never mind what she'd thought. She scoffed at herself, a sob escaping her lips. She covered her mouth with her hand. She should have kept to her usual practice. Fuck 'em, use 'em up and toss 'em. Men were only good for one thing and, predictably, Trent had proven that theory one more time.

Chapter Eleven

Trent felt like shit—and not because he had a sex hangover, although his body hurt like hell...sore in all the right places. It should have given him an ego stroke to know that he'd fucked Sabine to the point of muscle exhaustion. But he'd also fucked things up with her, big time, and all because of his stupid jealousy.

Adam was her bodyguard, right-hand man, rumored lover. Trent had seen it all over the deep web. He knew that Sabine treated Adam like more than just an employee, but there had been pictures to prove it, pictures more scandalous than the ones that had been leaked with him and Sabine. Adam was built like a brick house and probably cranked her in all the right ways too. And, he had access to her more than Trent did and was someone she trusted, liked and, apparently, fucked often.

When she'd mentioned his name, so casually after tossing out that she'd let Trent know if she screwed another guy, he'd just lost it in a flare of emotion that had made words fall out of his mouth with little control. Where had it come from? He wasn't going to lie. It had been brewing for days while she'd been gone and had been made worse by some tabloid articles he'd read about her that had made it seem like she was always on the hunt for new meat. On the one hand, it made him angry that the media always painted her as nothing but a whore. On the other hand, she did seem to have a trail of discarded men behind her. Adam, though, her trusted employee, was never one of the men who were tossed aside. He was special to her.

Trent's jealousy had been like a pressure cooker and her comment had made him blow.

He regretted it now, but he was too embarrassed to do anything about it. *What an absolute ass.* Not that he knew how to fix it even if he could… If she wanted him out of her life, he was out. Adam would make sure of it.

Fuck!

Trent didn't want to go home. He had a change of clothes at the office so he went there, regret hanging around his neck the entire way. M&M was a ghost town, as expected. It was after lunch hour on a Friday. Most of the executives left early, especially on long weekends. They were likely golfing together, drinking fifty-dollar-an-ounce whiskey and smoking hundred-dollar cigars, stroking each other's egos, living the life.

Trent was not living the life. He wasn't even close.

Pathetic.

All he wanted now was to shower, get the smell of Sabine off him so it would stop driving him mad and bury himself in work. That was what he did best — channel any emotional disruption into a kick-ass campaign. Not that he had anything pressing to work on right now... The last campaign he'd hit out of the park, Sabine had had a hand in.

Fuck, I'm such an idiot. If he thought begging forgiveness would work, he'd totally consider it.

The look in Sabine's eyes when she'd ordered him out of her place had told him that not even begging would do the trick. She had detached from him emotionally in that moment. It had been all over her face. She was done with him. And fuck if his heart didn't ache because of it. *Ache, shit...* It felt like the damn thing was shredded to bits and hanging there useless.

He stepped off the elevator, his thoughts on his colossal fuck up, his eyes on the floor, and almost took out Roy.

"Whoa there," Roy said, his hands out to brace himself against Trent. "Slow down!"

"Sorry, sir," Trent mumbled as he helped steady the other man's footing.

"Trent, well, aren't you the man of the hour?"

Trent froze. "The man of the hour?"

What were the odds of Roy knowing about his activities the night before? Trent had calculated the possibility and found that it was a relatively low risk. He knew that particular Kitty Calls Boutique wasn't well attended and it wasn't like Roy had any association with Sabine's companies. The man was a walking embodiment of all things family man. He went to church on Sundays with his wife of forty years. His three children, all still in universities across the country, had extensive experience with volunteer programs. As a family, they carried the brand of Morgan and Miller into their personal lives and beyond — outreach, charity, volunteerism. No vices. No scandal.

Roy snorted. "You just can't stay away from her, can you?"

Ah-h-h, shit.

"Oh, Trent, you're here!" Ellie came around the corner then, her purse on her shoulder. "Mr. Miller told me to go home, since you were out for the day." She winced a bit when she said that, so Trent knew it hadn't gone over well. "I can order us some lunch. Have you eaten?"

"No, Ellie, you go home," Roy said over his shoulder. "Trent and I have some business to discuss in my office. You won't be needed for the rest of the day."

That didn't sound good. Ellie's face mirrored Trent's, no doubt.

Ah-h-h-h, double shit.

I'm so getting fired.

"Thank you, sir," Ellie said, cringing as she passed Trent, a hand out to give him a reassuring pat. "Call me later, okay?"

Trent nodded. His gut twisted at the thoughts going through his head. *How did Roy figure it out? Did someone tell him? Sabine? No, fuck, why do I always suspect her of trying to ruin me?* He had trust issues. That was no excuse, though. He was acting like an asshole.

When he'd done extensive research into Sabine's Fuck Room, he'd discovered that she and her security team took a lot of precautions to protect their patrons — no cell phones, no technology to speak of, private membership and heavy vetting. There was always security watching the voyeurs. So not only did he know Sabine hadn't been taking a huge risk in exposing herself there with him, he also knew that they were pretty safe from a leak—or at least, he'd thought he'd known about that. Now he wasn't so sure.

Once Trent had snapped out of his thoughts, Roy was already halfway down the hall that led to his office. *Fuck me.*

Trent followed reluctantly. Roy had a finger on the pulse of all things Morgan and Miller. He knew what was happening in the staff's lives, sent flowers when someone had a relative pass, gave time off when there was too much stress rolling around, even paid medical bills for those who couldn't manage. He knew things—intimate, secret things that he always seemed to use for good. People loved him for that. Trent had never questioned it…until now.

So maybe Roy did know what was going on. Maybe he had ways of knowing, keeping an eye on his prize horse to make sure Trent didn't fuck up the reputation of M&M again. It wasn't like the man was without connections.

Roy was already pouring drinks by the time Trent made it down the hall and into his corner office. He passed a glass to Trent without a word then moved to his desk.

Trent set the booze aside, not feeling the need to numb his brain at the moment. There was nothing he could do to stop this train wreck from happening. He'd rather have his wits about him while his life derailed.

"Roy, I—"

"Take a look at this," Roy said, cutting him off while shoving a thick file across the desk to Trent.

Trent frowned, his eyes on the file. "What is it?" His thoughts immediately turned to surveillance, especially since he could see photos poking out from the bundle of papers. Was he being watched by some kind of private investigator?

"Sit, son." Roy's tone had lost some of its bite. He motioned to the chair next to Trent, taking a sip of his drink as he did. "I need you to see this."

With the sinking feeling worsening, Trent did as he was told. He pulled the chair closer and took a seat. Roy flipped the cover of the file open.

"As you know, Sabine and I have a history." He shuffled some of the papers aside. "Her father and I were very old friends. We started a business together, Excalibur Enterprises, specializing in security systems. We were young, built that business from the ground up."

Trent leaned forward, looking over the photos. Sabine was younger in them, probably in her early twenties. It was definitely during the party time of her life. In many of them she was with a guy who looked older than her. It was a familiar face that Trent couldn't quite place.

"That's Dylan, my eldest." Roy's voice cracked a bit as he said that. He took another sip of his drink.

"Dylan?"

Roy had three children—Katrina and Elle were twins, Thomas was the youngest. He'd never heard of Dylan.

"Yes, Dylan is my son from a previous relationship. I was young and careless back then. I fell in lust and got her pregnant. Dylan turned thirty-seven last year." Roy moved the photos again, shoving aside the ones of Sabine to settle on ones of Dylan, in a hospital bed, clearly ill and suffering. He'd lost weight from his previous photos, had deep, dark circles under his eyes. His cheeks looked gaunt and sunken. His hair was lank, unkempt and vacant looking, like he was haunted. "This is Dylan now."

"What happened?"

"Sabine happened," Roy spat. He adjusted his tie to loosen it then leaned back in his chair. "She destroyed him."

"Roy, I—"

"Listen to me, boy." Roy held his hand up. "I'm only telling you this because I care about what happens to you. You've got a future at Morgan and Miller—or anywhere else you want, if I'm going to be honest. You're brilliant with marketing and have sense for promotion that fits with the new world of all things social media and technology. I see you making partner here one day."

Trent blinked. Hard. *Um…what?*

"But not if that woman corrupts you." Roy got up and moved to the bar. "She and Dylan grew up together. Like I said, we were close, me and her father. And Sabine and Dylan were close too. They both grew up as our business was taking off, both indulged a little too much, spoiled by her father and me because we'd never had the things we wanted them to have. I'll take that part of the blame. We created these entitled kids and catered to their whims. When Sabine hit the teen years, she really started pushing boundaries, as I'm sure you've seen from the media exposure over the years."

Roy started drinking his new drink right at the bar. He picked up the bottle and brought it with him to the desk, choosing to sit on the edge rather than take his seat again. "Things got out of control with her quickly. I tried talking to her father, Bernard, but he would hear none of it. He cherished that girl. Her mother had died during childbirth and Bernard forever felt guilty about that. Sabine was leading Dylan down a dark path with her and I couldn't abide by it. That led to many, many fights between my old friend and me So much so that we ended up dissolving our partnership. We sold our company for a lot of money and went our separate ways."

He sighed then downed another drink before refilling his glass. Trent could see that this story was costing him. His body slumped, shoulders down, looking defeated.

"I did what I could to keep Dylan away from Sabine. I forbade him from seeing her. I sent him away time and time again—first to boarding school in England. She followed him there. Then to Australia for sailing courses... She found him there too. Every place, no matter how far I sent him, she followed. And because her father indulged her, she had money and resources to break my son out. Even when I had security with him at all times, she still managed to get her way. And my son, Dylan? He was enamored with her, of course—just as you are.

"Her father got ill...very ill. His new business, Cowan Enterprises, was faltering after years and years of limited success. I took pity on my old friend and offered to come to his aid, to help him sort out the creditors who were threatening to take everything. I did what I could, but his health was too far gone and he was gravely ill. When he died, Sabine lashed out, mostly at me. She took over her father's company and turned it into the blasphemy that it is today, obliterating everything that man had built. But that wasn't enough for her. She wanted revenge, thinking that I had something to do with her father's death. So she went after Dylan. She plied him with sex and drugs, gave him attention then took it away. She flaunted her other relationships and, ultimately, she destroyed him. He overdosed on drugs that I'm assuming she supplied, and now he's here, in a private care facility, his mind utterly obliterated."

"Sabine wouldn't do that," Trent blurted.

Roy frowned, looking more troubled by Trent's statement than the story he'd just told. "Oh no?" He reached over and shuffled through the photos again, pulling out an envelope from within. Inside were more pictures. "Do you recognize this guy?"

It was Adam, Sabine's bodyguard. The photos showed him passing small packages to Dylan and looking very much like a drug dealer. There were other pictures where Adam and Dylan were sitting on a couch, at a party, snorting powder together.

"They got him hooked on meth then they took pictures of him using." He took out a handwritten note that was paperclipped to a series of photos of Dylan using drugs.

Roy,
Thought you should know.
S

"She threatened to release this to the press. Threatened to destroy me with the scandal. She didn't know I was surveilling her and her fucker of a bodyguard at the same time." He reached over and pulled his laptop closer, typing in a few things before turning it completely. A news report came up. "I turned what I had over to police."

Roy hit Play.

"Adam Lancaster, arrested on drug trafficking charges last Tuesday, was released from custody today. His employer, Sabine Cowan, posted bail."

Roy hit pause then flipped to another video.

"CEO of Kitty Calls, Sabine Cowan, made a statement yesterday denying her involvement with long-time on-again, off-again boyfriend Dylan Miller and the allegations that her bodyguard was supplying him with drugs."

"It is my understanding," Sabine said, her eyes locked on the camera, *"that Dylan Miller has been a drug abuser for some time. If you are looking for someone to blame for that, I'd be looking closer to home. His father is more concerned with maintaining his reputation than helping his son."*

Roy hit pause. "Dylan saw this." Roy took another drink. "He panicked. He didn't want me to know what was going on—not realizing, of course, that I already did. So he overdosed on meth. Whether it was attempted suicide or an attempted escape from reality, I don't know. I'll never know. The housekeeper found him. He was in a coma for weeks. When he came around, he was essentially a vegetable."

He showed another video, this one brief—a statement about Roy's son nearly dying from a drug overdose. But what was worse was that the coverage to follow was of Sabine at a gala event, time-stamped the next night, showing her and Adam, arm in arm, walking the red carpet like they were a couple, laughing and smiling for the cameras.

"She didn't blink when she heard about Dylan. She didn't come to the hospital. She didn't care." Roy growled. "But she was responsible for it all." He pulled out a card from the file.

The cover had a bouquet of flowers and the inscription on the inside read, *"I told you so. S"*

The same elegant lines and a signature that anyone would recognize as belonging to Sabine.

"She did this to Dylan." Roy put the card down on his desk. "And she'll do it to you. If you have any doubts that she leaked that video of you, I hope they're gone. She's capable of worse. The more you engage with her, the worse it will get. She's a predator. She knows how to target men's weaknesses. She's built an empire on it. She's always looking for ways to destroy me too, and I'm afraid I got you caught up in this nasty business." Roy leaned forward and gripped Trent's shoulder. "I'm sorry for that. But, Trent, I refuse to let her do to you what she did to my son. Her hatred for me, however misplaced, knows no bounds, and she will use you to get to me, especially because she knows how much I value you."

Trent's mind was reeling. *Can this be true?* The evidence was certainly damning. "She said she didn't leak that video." His voice trembled, the words sounding hollow, even to himself.

Roy sighed then pulled his phone out and passed it to Trent. He didn't have to watch the video to know what Roy was showing him.

"Where'd you get this?" Trent asked him.

It was from the night before, explicit video of him and Sabine, their faces exposed. His heart was in his throat.

"Where do you think?" Roy scoffed. "Sabine is one of the most cunning liars I have ever known and she won't stop until she's destroyed you." He leaned back, standing so that he could walk to the other side of his desk. "I've purchased a plane ticket and made arrangements for you to fly home."

"Fly home? To Colorado?"

Roy was reaching into his desk drawer. "Yes, to get you out of here. After last night, I'm trying to do damage control as we speak. We need to keep that out of the media as well." He slid the ticket across the desk. "Let me help you with this mess. It's the least I can do." He paused. "But, son, I need you to promise me you'll stay away from that woman."

Trent's face was on fire, the reality of the situation sinking in. His heart was in his throat. He couldn't speak, so he nodded.

"For your parents' sake, let me handle this for you. I have experience with Sabine and her treachery. Go home and reassess your priorities. Come back next week. I'll have everything taken care of by then."

"Roy, I'm—"

Roy raised his hand. "You remind me of Dylan, and I have a soft spot for you. Sabine is a cruel woman with no heart. I'm sorry you got tangled up with her. That's on me. I should never have sent you to her in the first place. Please, take the ticket. Go home. Let me clean up this mess, then you can get back to work and move on with your life."

Trent felt about an inch tall. He could have argued that it was all his fault, that he had been the one who'd taken Sabine to that club the previous night and that he'd known there was a risk of exposure. But he was too tired and too confused to do much more than nod, taking the ticket as he stood. "Thank you, sir."

And that's how your life comes crashing down around you.

Chapter Twelve

"That bastard!" Sabine replayed the video. "Adam! Get in here!"

She'd buried herself in work all day after Trent had left her place, trying to get him out of her head and, as impossible as had it turned out to be, out of her heart as well. It had been three days...three torturous days where she'd checked her phone liked an obsessed stalker waiting for something to come from Trent. He'd been silent...which reinforced her need to be silent...so no one was talking and Sabine was cycling through all the ways she'd fucked things up.

"What's up, boss?" Adam came strolling in, his face set with a look of concern.

"Roy Miller is what's up." She turned her computer toward Adam. "There's a video from the other night."

"Not possible." Adam leaned in and watched only part of the video, his expression changing from denial to shock — just a flicker, though, then it was gone. "I had eyes on all those guys in there that night. No one had technology for recording."

"You had eyes on, looking for the usual tricks. Roy went above and beyond this time." She laughed bitterly. "I don't care what comes out about me. Feed the beast." Good or bad publicity... If it had to do with sex, it only helped her bottom line. "It's not just me he's threatening to expose." And that was what was really bothering her.

"What does he want?" Adam straightened.

Because they both knew he was after something more than just releasing a scandalous video.

"The same thing he's always wanted — me behind bars, my company destroyed." And Trent was caught up in the middle of it all. Collateral damage.

"If he exposes you, he exposes Trent as well. That will damage M&M to some degree. Both of your faces are clear in this video." Adam pulled his phone out. "I'm going to call my contacts at the PD to see if he's reached out to them."

She wasn't going to lie — the Kitty Calls that the public saw was nothing compared to the Kitty Calls that existed in the shadows, riding the line of legal and illegal when it came to the sexual exploits of her clients. She took precautions, of course, and she had a lot of people in her pocket, but that didn't mean that she wasn't untouchable. "Yes, give Ted a call. Ask him to dig around a bit. Oh, and let him know that everything is set for his son's bachelor party next weekend."

Adam smiled knowingly. *Men and their trysts.* She could count on them to look down their noses at her business practices, while at the same time, utilize her services. Adam nodded then left, his phone already pressed to his ear.

"Ted, buddy, how's it going?" He closed the door behind him.

She wasn't worried so much about herself. She had a powerful lawyer on retainer for this kind of thing. She wouldn't see an hour behind bars. But she knew Roy would take Trent out in his attempt to get her, and that was not something she could abide. The man was ruthless with his moral high-horse persona. He'd even sacrificed his own son in an attempt to bring Sabine down.

He'd wanted her dad's company — to absorb it into Morgan and Miller when her father died. And Roy had expected her to just roll over and let him have it. But she'd made a promise to her dad that it would never happen, so she'd stepped up and taken control. Roy hadn't liked that. There had been bad blood between them for a while, that was true. She'd been wild as a teen. Roy felt that she'd corrupted his son, Dylan, when the reality was that he, the older, wiser, rich brat, had led her down many dark paths as well. She wasn't going to claim innocence, but she wasn't the total villain that Roy wanted everyone to believe she was.

Dylan had made bad choices. He and Adam had done some stupid shit together. Adam had been his bodyguard first, hired by his dad, something Roy had probably never forgiven himself for. Then they had been lovers, Dylan and Adam. They'd partied hard, even when she hadn't been around, even after she'd taken Adam on as her security, pulling him away from Dylan in an attempt to save them both. She hadn't realized how bad it was getting until the photos had surfaced showing Dylan and Adam together, snorting something very illegal. That had threatened her business in a way that she couldn't spin. Sex was one thing, but drugs? Yeah, that was crossing a line.

But unlike Dylan, Adam had accepted Sabine's help when she'd offered, getting him into a rehab program to clean up before the drugs completely consumed him. Dylan had made a different choice. And although she mourned the loss of her childhood friend, his downward spiral had more to do with his controlling ass of a father than anything Sabine had ever done with him. Rebellion had been Dylan's highest priority. Whatever he knew would hurt his father most, he did it—even at the cost of his own life. He'd set up an elaborate scene, drugging himself to the point of overdose, hoping his father would rescue him. That had never happened. Dylan's actions had caused everyone to suffer, her included.

You gotta cut those people loose from your life, ya know? She'd done what she could to try to help him but he didn't want her help. He'd wanted his father's help, but the man had been much too busy with his new family and his squeaky-clean reputation to bother with his first-born, beyond sticking him in an out-of-the-way facility where he'd spend the rest of his life wasting away and forgotten. The doctors had said that with the right treatment, Dylan could recover some of his faculties. Maybe not be as he was before, but he could regain awareness, maybe speech too. Roy hadn't explored those options. So now, Dylan was essentially a vegetable, rotting away on painkillers while he drooled all over himself.

Sabine had shed her tears. She'd railed against the injustice of it all. But the reality was that life wasn't always fair and people had to accept things that happened and move on. So that was what she'd done and so had Roy. They hadn't been that different in the end.

She picked up her phone and scrolled to Trent's number. She wanted to warn him, give him a heads-up about his mentor. She didn't know exactly what Roy was up to, but there had to be a purpose behind him sending her the video. She hovered her finger over his name, ready to hit Call. But she hesitated. She was still angry as hell with him. His jealous outburst was shit that she just didn't put up with. His accusations were out of line as well.

It was possible that she'd been a bit too harsh with him, though, and a bit too callous with her comments. Telling him in such a flippant way that she'd let him know if she was going to have sex outside of their relationship, when sleeping with another person was the last thing she wanted to do. Trent wasn't from her world and he wasn't like the other men she'd been with over the years. She could probably have been gentler with him, soothed his anxiety instead of stoking it. Maybe she could have opened herself up and told him how she really felt instead of hiding behind her fucked-up bravado. So he'd gotten into her heart? What was wrong with that?

She sighed. Fine, so she owned him an apology. She went ahead and hit his name on her phone. It went straight to voicemail.

"Hi Trent, it's Sabine. I really need to talk to you. Please call me back when you get this." She ended the call.

"Hey, Sabine." Adam came into her office. "Ted is going to do some sniffing around but there's nothing going on in his department. He hasn't heard from Roy."

Okay, so what's the old bastard up to?

"You might want to give Sam Henderson a call," Adam continued, reading her thoughts.

She was already lifting her phone to her ear, Sam's number on speed dial.

If there was a story brewing, Sam would know about it.

"Sabine, to what do I owe this pleasure?" Sam answered after the first ring, the background noise of traffic suggesting he was downtown.

"Sam, you have time for a meeting with me?"

Sam paused. "I'm on assignment right now. Got to do some running around."

"That assignment doesn't have anything to do with me, does it?"

"No, should it?" Sam laughed awkwardly then sighed. "Not everything is about you, Sabine." He covered the phone to speak to someone else. "Fine, I'll meet you in the usual place. Give me twenty minutes."

Sam Henderson was a long-time friend of Sabine's and a hard-hitting reporter. He didn't promise to keep her out of his stories. Dirt was dirt and reporters needed to keep the public in a feeding frenzy, but he wasn't out to get her, either. As much as she could trust the media, Sam was one of the better guys. That didn't mean he pulled punches, but he usually gave her a heads up when they were about to hit.

Twenty minutes later, they were seated in their usual back booth at a run-down little diner that was better when someone had a hangover rather than when they were looking to fill their stomach on any other occasion. Sabine was nursing a tea, her stomach not really in the mood for anything heavier.

"Things have died down for you since the Morgan and Miller fiasco." Sam wasn't hedging for information. He was stating a fact.

Sabine cocked an eyebrow. "That just so happens to be what I'm here to talk to you about."

"I'm not giving you names or breaking the confidence of my sources."

That was Sam's typical conversation starter.

"But I did do a bit of digging when I got off the phone with you. There's been some chatter about your New Jersey Boutique. I don't know what it is exactly, but there's a buzz. Would you care to fill me in? Give me an exclusive?" He wagged his eyebrows. "I've heard things about that place."

Sabine cocked hers. "No."

It wasn't totally unexpected that he was hearing chatter. If they had the video, there'd be more of a buzz, though. Sabine took a sip of her tea. It was bitter. She picked up the container of sugar and stirred some in. "I need to know if you've heard anything from Roy Miller."

"Good old Roy?" he snorted. "Not recently."

"He emailed a compromising video of me — or at least what he thinks is one — along with a veiled threat."

"Again?" Sam whistled. "He hasn't given up yet?"

The waitress came with Sam's order — a burger and fries. It looked appetizing, but Sabine wouldn't fall for it, despite how enticing the smell might be. Sabine knew from experience that it would sit in her stomach like a rock for the rest of the day. And the way her gut was churning, it was better to stick with the tea.

Sam waited for the server to leave. "You got something going on with that guy, Trent whatever? Roy's golden boy? Does he mean something to you?"

Trent whatever. As if he didn't know exactly what was going on. She raised an eyebrow again and Sam chuckled. This wasn't just fishing. Sam *did* know something.

"You can't blame a guy for asking. Inquiring minds want to know." He picked up a couple of fries and shoved them into his mouth. "It just seems to me that you're tied up with Roy over this kid he's mentoring. Sounds like a familiar story to me."

The look he gave her was defiant. He knew that Dylan was off limits for conversation.

Sabine pursed her lips.

"Sheesh, relax. I'm just toeing the line." He took a bite of his burger.

"You released that video, right? Of me and Trent at my Kitty Cat party a few weeks ago."

Sam didn't stop eating. He picked up more fries with one hand, while still taking bites of his burger. "Yeah, it was sent to me anonymously." He shrugged. "I actually kind of thought *you* had leaked it. I made some good cash on that. Someone was very generous. You sure you don't want something to eat? I'm buying." He winked.

Sabine shook her head. "No, thanks and no, I didn't leak the video. But I have a feeling I know who did."

Sam stopped chewing, his eyes going wide. "Oh yeah, enlighten me. That shit was gold."

"You have no soul, do you?" Sabine scoffed.

Sam shrugged. "You know this about me." He put his burger down. "I'll sacrifice whomever I need to get the story out. The truth is the truth. So, who's the source? You got Adam on it, don't you? What'd he find out?"

"Nothing concrete, but I'm thinking the only person who has something to gain from all this is Roy."

"Roy Miller? Nah." He choked a bit as he swallowed his food. "Why would he purposely try to ruin the golden boy of M&M? The company is just regaining their footing."

"I don't know, but I won't be surprised if the video he sent me today ends up on all the news channels at six tonight."

Sam frowned. "I haven't heard anything about it." He pointed at her. "Give it to me and I'll spin it away from you."

Was it possible that Sam was out of the loop? Unlikely. "Uh, no." Sabine wasn't going to trust Sam with information like that. "I'll take my chances."

"Sabine...after all our years together?" He whined mockingly between slurps of his drink.

"Roy is up to something." She took another sip of tea. The sugar didn't help, and now it was too cool to enjoy. She set it aside with a grimace. Roy had wanted her to sign a confidentiality agreement for the CFO, Harold McKibbon, to keep his affairs covered up. He'd sent Trent as a decoy. Sabine felt certain of that. He couldn't have known that Sabine would invite Trent back to her party...or that things would get sexual between them. But he might have baited her just to see if she would. She reflected on that. Maybe she was more predictable where men were concerned than she thought. Maybe Roy had her pegged. He'd sent her a tasty little treat and she'd gobbled him up.

Sabine gulped, a split-second thought turning to Trent. Maybe he was in on it? Her stomach churned. *No. Sabine, no.* He was too innocent...too open. She shut down all thoughts of Trent. It wasn't good for her heart and she refused to believe that he would willfully set her up for a fall.

Sam's phone dinged. He glanced down at it, frowned, then picked it up to read the texts coming in. "Hey, I gotta run." He dug a few bills out of his pocket and threw them down on the table.

"What's the hurry?"

He slid out of the booth then paused, looking a little torn. "There's a story breaking. Nothing to do with you. But hey, I'll throw you a bone. One of the photographers I work with told me that your boy, Trent, hopped on a plane a couple of days ago, headed to Colorado. He thought there might be a story there but his editor wouldn't let him pursue it. I didn't think much of it either. Don't his parents live out there?" Sam shrugged. "You change your mind about letting me in on the story and I'm a phone call away."

Sabine waved him off. *Thanks but no thanks.*

He left and Sabine stayed put.

Why would Trent go home? Had Roy fired him? Had he been all torn up over their fight? She wanted to think that she was just that important to him, but it didn't sit right, not completely. Once again she felt like Roy had something to do with this.

She picked up her phone and tried Trent's number. It went straight to voicemail...again. So she dialed Morgan and Miller.

"Trent Brooks, please." It was Monday. He should be back in his office, unless he really was back home in Colorado.

"Good morning, Mr. Brooks isn't in today. Can I take a message?"

"No message, but I'm wondering if you could tell me how I might reach Mr. Brooks. He's working on something for me and I have information he needs."

"Oh, well, are you sure about that? I didn't think he had any projects pending." The woman hesitated, her voice catching. "His calendar is clear for the rest of this week."

Sabine guessed by her sweet voice that this was Ellie, the super-star secretary that Trent often talked about. He'd said that Ellie managed his work life like a pro, so of course she knew exactly what was going on with his calendar.

"Do you know when he'll be back?"

Another long pause. "I can't say for sure. Maybe you should try calling his cell phone? He's usually pretty good about returning calls."

There was an awkwardness to the way she was speaking, like she knew Trent wouldn't be taking calls or returning them. "Thanks... I'll try that."

Sabine hung up. Had he been fired? Was that what the awkwardness was all about?

She scrolled through her phone until she found Roy's personal number. Desperate times... She didn't actually think he would answer, but he did.

"I have nothing more to say to you, Sabine."

"Roy, where's Trent? Did you fire him?"

"You leave that boy alone, Sabine. Haven't you destroyed enough lives?"

"I'm not buying it, Roy. What are you after?" She tapped her fingers on the table then regretted it immediately. It was sticky as hell. She grabbed a napkin and dipped it in the water to wipe her fingers. "You sent Trent to me on purpose. You knew I'd be intrigued. So, what's the game, Roy? I know you released those photos and the video of Trent and me at the party. I just can't figure out why."

"Delusions. You and your paranoia. You can't figure out why because it's another one of your myths that you've created in your deluded brain. Trent needs some time away from you, Sabine. I told him what you did to Dylan."

Told him what I did? His version of things. Trent's doubts about her would have made him a believer if Roy had told the story the way he understood it. She was always the villain in Roy's mind. Her gut twisted with rage.

"Did you tell him what *you* did, old man?"

His version of the story would have left out a lot of incriminating evidence about his own negligent actions toward his first-born.

"I've got Trent's best interests at heart, unlike you. I won't let his life be destroyed by your carelessness, your callousness." He cleared his throat.

"I'm not the one leaking compromising videos, Roy!" Her voice was loud enough to raise a few eyebrows. She got up from the booth and walked to the back of the restaurant, where there were no patrons.

There was a pause, long enough to make her think he'd hung up on her.

"I actually believe you when you say that." He laughed cruelly. "If you're looking for a leak, maybe you should look close to home, as you like to say. Instead of pointing fingers at me, maybe you should look to your closest allies and consider the possibility that your trust is misplaced and you've got your information mixed up. It wouldn't be the first time. What you have to ask yourself is… Who has motive *and* opportunity? While I admit seeing your company fail would give me great satisfaction, I'm smart enough to know that that's not going to happen with scandalous videos. Your adoring public would just eat that shit up, you filthy whore."

He hung up.

You filthy whore. Somehow, when Roy said it, it actually made her feel shame. And that pissed her off more than anything else.

Her mind whirled. Her closest allies — Adam, Sam, Lexi. What if? *No.* She wouldn't go down that road. That was what Roy did. He turned people against one another. Divide and conquer.

Sabine slid into another booth, the fight suddenly slipping out of her. She was tired. This game was exhausting and she fucking missed Trent.

She needed to figure out her next move, but suddenly she felt like her tethers were failing and she was loose in the wind.

The people who were closest to her were beyond suspicion and her accusations always turned to Roy.

But his words kept rolling in her head. Who had motive and opportunity? Who would she suspect the least?

What if she should have been paying closer attention to those who had opportunity, even if she couldn't see the motive?

Ugh. Her head hurt. She needed time to think and the world felt like it was closing in on her.

She looked up a number she didn't use *ever*, then put the phone to her ear.

"Hi, yes, I need to book a flight for tonight. Yes, Colorado."

Chapter Thirteen

Roy had advised him to stay a little longer in Colorado while he dealt with things. Trent had decided to heed his advice. For the first few days he'd caught himself looking over his shoulder for a media van or paparazzi, expecting the worst. If his parents had picked up on his paranoia, they hadn't said anything. Instead, they'd put him to work—not questioning why he was there beyond his hastily explained vacation time, just happy that he was. They were getting older, and working long hours at the meat shop was grueling at times. Seeing that he was an only child, there wasn't anyone to leave the business to, either. Unless Trent really did lose his job. Then perhaps he'd be venturing into a different career path.

He didn't mind the work. It wasn't his ideal profession, true, but being back home was familiar territory. His mind needed a break from the whirlwind of excitement he'd been living for weeks now. Butchering was messy and didn't smell the greatest at times, but it was methodical. It didn't require much thinking, just doing. And he could get lost in the movements of it, numbing his mind.

Not thinking about Sabine. *Not much anyway.*

Okay, that was a lie. He thought about her almost every minute. He missed her. He wanted to call her. But he'd kept his phone off, as per Roy's instructions. He didn't know what hell was waiting for him back in New York, and being unplugged as he was at his folks' place kept his sanity in check — for the most part, anyway. He knew nothing good would come from turning his phone on. He had enough willpower to keep it off and he certainly didn't need the Internet to keep him occupied. His memories were torturing him enough with that.

Sabine crawling toward me on all fours, her tits swaying, her hips moving, her lips curled into a wicked smile.

Sabine's lips on my dick, sucking back my cum with those delicious moans of hers. Purring against my skin so that my whole body hummed.

Tied up and blindfolded, trusting me to do her right. To make her explode with pleasure.

Yeah, his mind was filled with those kind of thoughts, making him zone out at work, at home and at the dinner table while his mom was talking about the latest books she'd gotten at the library. It had been embarrassing when he'd had to excuse himself to rub one out. He was masturbating at least three times a day.

But that wasn't why he missed her — well, not only that. He loved talking to her, hearing about her day and finding out about the new ideas she had brewing. He found her inspirational. She stoked his creativity. He ached to be near her, if only to smell her, touch her, whisper with her.

He sighed then continued to tear the membrane off the ribs he was prepping. They were a special order for a party. He'd offered to work in the back so that his dad could deal with customers. He just wasn't in the mood to chit chat with the locals, pretending to be happy to be home when all he really wanted to do was race back to the city and find Sabine, then beg her for forgiveness.

He tossed the ribs into the bin for marinating then moved on to the next rack.

He'd be back in the city soon enough, plugged in to all the news. Then he'd hear what he'd missed. He'd started the week thinking only about how Roy was going to fix things for him, keep him in the job and out of the media. He'd been grateful for the opportunity to stay clear of it all. But then those Sabine thoughts kept invading...circling doubts about the story Roy had told, about Sabine's involvement with his son — whether or not she could be capable of the malicious things Roy was accusing her of. His brain was a muddled mess and he didn't know who to count on and who to put faith in, which was probably part of his problem. Maybe his tragic flaw was that he felt compelled to trust people completely. To see past their faults.

The bell on the shop's door rang, snapping him back to his job at hand.

"Hello, Miss. What can I help you with today?" His father's booming voice floated close to the pass-through window as he walked past.

"Yes, hi, Mr. Brooks. I'm actually looking for Trent. I'm a friend of his from New York. Is he here?"

Trent froze. *Sabine.* His heart ramped up. A sweat broke out on his forehead. His stomach pitched. *Why is she here?*

"Trent, son, you've got a visitor." His dad pushed through the swinging door. "There's a beautiful woman out there." He chuckled, waving Trent away from the meat. "Take that apron off and wash your hands. I'll do the rest."

For a split second he actually thought about asking his dad to tell her to go. He didn't want to face her, to be humiliated all over again. Her being there couldn't be good, right? He sighed. *Stop being an asshole. Man up.*

He passed the knife to his dad and moved quickly to clean himself up, checking himself in the mirror to make sure there wasn't any blood on his face. There was something about being in this place that always made him feel so country, so homely looking. That was the exact opposite of how he was in the city. But there was nothing he could do about that now, though.

"She must be someone special, huh, son?" his dad said as he was passing, a sly grin on his face.

Someone special. Yeah. That's an understatement.

She had her back to him when he pushed through the swinging door, but even so, he was drawn to the presence of her. She was wearing casual clothes, not the norm for Sabine. Her usual flowing wispy blouse, tight pencil skirt and impossibly high heels were replaced with worn-in jeans, a T-shirt and a baseball cap. Her hair was in a ponytail, swaying as she moved from one display case to the next. It was an effective disguise. No one would ever guess that Sabine Cowan was the dressed-down, no-fuss woman browsing in a butcher shop in Colorado. He hadn't thought it would ever be possible for her to blend in, but here she was, acting normal, looking like one of the locals. She looked very country but in no way homely.

"Do people actually buy cow tongue?" She didn't look up or turn around. She just tapped the glass with her nail.

"Yes, it sells." He came around the counter and cleared his throat. "What are you doing here, Sabine?" Seeing her conjured a few different emotions. On the one hand, he wanted to pull her into an embrace and kiss away their fight. On the other, he wanted to question her about Roy's accusations, demand to know what had happened between her and Dylan.

He did neither and just stood there like a damned idiot.

She turned then, a small smile there and gone as she did. "I came to see you."

"To see *me*?" He shook his head, his heart hammering harder. "Sabine—"

"I know that Roy told you about Dylan." She had her hand raised. "I'd just like you to hear my side of things before you make any lasting judgments."

"What difference does it make?" She had no reason to explain things to him. He was easily discarded, pushed aside for the next guy. *Come on...* Sabine was one of the sexiest women alive. What did she care about his judgment?

She's here, dumbass, he reminded himself. *She's here...in Colorado. Open your mouth and apologize. Make it right. Stop being a giant baby.*

"Of course it makes a difference." Her eyes grew wide for a moment but then that smile was back, making her look sweet and oh-so-tempting. "I want you in my life for as long as I can have you."

"So this isn't about some need for revenge on Roy? Trying to strip my loyalty away from him for some game you're playing?" *Shut up!* His mouth was on impulse, his thoughts rolling out with little control. He crossed his arms. "Because that's what he wants me to believe." And the truth was, Trent didn't know *what* to believe. That had been the most frustrating part of his whirling thoughts over the past few days. Sabine was important to him, but how much of what she said and did could he trust? Just because he wanted her in his life didn't mean she was good for him.

Wasn't that what Roy was trying to teach him?

"I know he does." Sabine sighed. "He's a man with a powerful presence and he's led you to believe that you owe him for your success. I've known Roy my whole life. I know how good he is at manipulating people into getting what he wants."

"I'm not being manipulated," Trent snapped.

"Why are you here, Trent? Because Roy told you to go home? Did you stop to wonder why he would want you gone?"

"To get away from you," Trent blurted, covering up for the realization that Sabine was right and he had just blindly followed Roy's instructions, not questioning things in the least. He'd assumed the worst about Sabine and taken Roy at his word once again.

She flinched. It was subtle but it was there, and he regretted his choice of words.

"He showed me a video of us at the club. He said you sent it to him." It sounded lame as Trent said it.

"You're always doubting me."

She had a sad kind of smile on her face that really broke his heart, like she was used to everyone thinking that about her. The world always underestimated Sabine Cowan — and now he had too.

"But you never stopped to question why *I* would do something like that."

145

Because you've done it before. To Dylan. Because I believed Roy's story that you hated him so much that you want to tarnish anything he cherishes. Because I'm a total asshole, just like the rest of the assholes you've tossed aside.

"You tell me again that Roy isn't a master manipulator when all he's done for you is give you a job, and here you are following his orders like he's the king of your world. You know you could get a job anywhere, right, Trent? You were the top of your class and the lead on a marketing campaign that rescued Morgan and Miller from obscurity. He wants you to think that you owe him something, but really, it's him who owes you." She had a fierce glint in her eyes. "And at no time did you give me the benefit of the doubt. You just assumed that someone like me would only be out to hurt you."

"He has a file, this thick, about you and Dylan and what went on."

"And I'm telling you, there's still more to the story than what he told you." She raised her hands, her tone softening. "Listen, Trent. I want a chance to explain, but I'm not going to force it on you. I'm staying at the Chatterly Inn for the night. I've got a flight for tomorrow. If you want to give me a chance to tell my side of the story, then meet me for dinner tonight at the hotel restaurant — at seven."

He knew going to that hotel would be a mistake. There would be no way he'd have the willpower to leave at the end of dinner. He wanted to be with her, even just in her presence, for as long as he could before he lost her forever. Yet he was too terrified to utter those words, so instead he said, "I'll think about it." And could have kicked himself in the ass.

She nodded. "Okay, but while you're thinking about it, why don't you read what's on here?" She pulled a USB out of her pocket. "I'm going to warn you that this may change your understanding of things beyond our relationship, though."

He took the USB, his fingers brushing hers. As corny as it sounded, he seriously felt like an electric pulse went through him at the contact. He so badly wanted to take her hand, to feel her skin. Instead, he held the USB up. "What's on it?"

She shrugged. "If Roy insists on speaking on my behalf, then I'll do the same. You should know just what kind of man you're dealing with."

"Sabine, I'm not interested in getting tangled up in this war between you two."

"Oh, sweetie, you're already a piece on the game board. I'm just trying to make sure you don't get knocked out without knowing what's really going on."

She turned and left. He wanted to chase after her. He had that impulse again. He wanted to kiss her, to touch her, to be with her. She was here, in his hometown. That meant something, didn't it? Yes, he decided. It meant something. If he was just a toss-away, she wouldn't have come. It wouldn't have mattered.

Trent moved to the window and watched as she got into a compact economy car, also a surprising revelation. She was going out of her way to look inconspicuous. He looked up and down the street then back to the car. She was alone in there. *No Adam.* So she'd traveled without her muscle? Another surprise.

"Who was that, son?" His dad came out of the back room carrying a tray of wings and pretending like he hadn't been listening the whole time.

"She's just a girl I know…from the city." Of course his dad had no idea who Sabine was. His parents took little interest in celebrity gossip. The only way they had even found out about his scandalous night at the Kitty Cat party was because of some gossiping customers who had felt the need to share the news. Trent wanted to brush off the visit and tell his dad that she was no one important, but he couldn't spit out that lie. Instead, Trent slipped the USB into his pocket and turned to help his dad restock the display cases.

He didn't think he wanted to see what was on the memory stick, but at the same time, he knew he didn't want to close the door on his relationship with Sabine without having all the information. He'd heard Roy out. He'd done what the man had said, had followed orders without question. Sabine was right about that. Now he needed to hear what she had to say.

* * * *

A few hours later, after he'd sent his folks out for a dinner on him, Trent sat at his desk staring at the computer, wondering what the fuck he was looking at. Or rather, if he was really seeing what he thought he was seeing.

He hadn't known Harold McKibbon at all, for that matter, other than chatting with the man briefly at meetings. He'd had no idea, of course, that the man had been using Sabine's services until after his untimely death. And he'd been so caught up in doing his job, namely getting Sabine to sign a confidentiality agreement, that he hadn't thought beyond that.

Sabine had given him a lot to digest — a lot to read, a lot to unravel. And his stomach was literally in knots over it.

Harold wasn't the only one involved with Kitty Calls. By the looks of things, it was Roy who had been making the arrangements.

Roy, the man who looked down on Sabine and condemned her business, had been setting up the CFO of his company to use her services.

It was almost too much to comprehend.

It made Trent's mind swirl around all the things he thought he'd known — all the truths he'd built his perceptions on regarding Roy and Morgan and Miller.

It made him regret, in so many ways, how he'd doubted Sabine.

And it made him pick up his phone, turn it on and call Ellie.

"Trent! How are you?" She sounded like she was out of breath, moving down the sidewalk, no doubt, on her way home.

"Hi, Ellie, I'm good. You?" He flicked the laptop screen closed and checked the time. It was already after seven. *Shit. I'm late.* "Listen. I'm sorry to interrupt," he continued, "but I have a favor to ask."

He wasn't going to tell her about what was going on. There was no sense in dragging her into the mess.

"Sure, Trent, whatever you need."

"Could you stop by my place tonight? Get a file for me from my desk?"

"A file? Sure. What am I looking for?"

He winced. He really didn't want to get her involved, but he wanted his hands on that file. "It's a red file labeled 'Backups'." He hesitated. "Don't read it. Okay?"

There was a pause then an awkward laugh. "Of course I won't. Do you want me to courier it to you?"

"Yes, please. Tonight, if possible. Whatever the cost, just put it on my account. I need it for the morning, okay?"

"Sure thing, boss. Consider it done."

"Great. Thanks, Ellie. You're the best. I gotta run. Talk to you soon, and thanks again!" Trent sucked in deep breath, then let it out after disconnecting the call.

He had something that Sabine needed to see and he knew it was going to change the game, as she called it, *permanently*.

Chapter Fourteen

She'd been stood up before — though that might be surprising to some. She hadn't really expected for Trent to do it to her, though. And the pain that caused was also unexpected — the depth of it anyway. She felt the rejection in a way that she hadn't for a long time. Trent's small-town innocence, while annoying where Roy was concerned, was too endearing in general to just toss away. And the fact that he wouldn't give her another chance, even after the information she'd given him, was really hurtful.

Unless, of course, he hadn't actually read the files on the USB. She sighed, sipped her wine and checked her phone for the time again. *Seven-thirty.*

She was willing to give it another half hour, she decided, then she'd give it up and go to her room.

She wasn't the kind of woman to force someone to stay with her. She knew what that felt like, and she had vowed a long time ago not to put that on someone else. So, she wouldn't call him, wouldn't go to him again.

She'd just wait, sitting alone in the quaint little small-town restaurant, drinking the house red — which at six dollars a glass was the most expensive alcohol on their bar menu — and thinking about all the things that had happened and feeling a bit too sorry for herself.

She'd fucked things up with Trent, but he wasn't the only thing on her mind.

There was also Adam.

She'd taken him for granted, sure, but what was worse was that she'd fallen for Roy's manipulation, even though it had been for only a short time, just as she'd accused Trent of doing to her. She'd left town without a word to Adam, doubting that he was trustworthy — and why? Because she'd put stock in Roy's accusations. Where the videos were coming from was a mystery, but the best person to figure it out was Adam. He wasn't the source. She knew that in her heart. Roy was very skilled at manipulation, taking those niggling doubts that had sat at the back of her thoughts and nudging them enough to bring them to the front. He was gifted at suggestion. That was what made him successful in PR, and that was what her dad had always warned her about. Roy could make a person believe the unbelievable. She'd forgotten that and cursed herself for falling for it. But it helped her to accept that if she'd fallen for it, then that was why Trent, who idolized the man, would fall for it as well.

She picked at the fresh bread roll on her plate. She'd held off on ordering and didn't feel all that hungry, but she knew some food would likely do her good. She opened the menu to look for the millionth time.

She'd called Adam when she'd landed at the airport, explained to him what she was up to then tasked him with getting to the bottom of things. Roy was covering something up and somehow Trent was tangled in it.

She'd apologize later to Adam for her temporary suspicion of him — maybe not in words, but she would make sure Adam knew that he was cherished. It was cowardly, perhaps, but Adam didn't really need to know her moments of doubt. All he needed to know was that he was valued.

She finished her glass of red and motioned to the waiter, ready to tell him that she would be eating in her room, when Trent walked in. He literally took her breath away.

His hair was damp, the curls combed down and darker than when his hair was dry. He'd shaven and was wearing well-worn jeans that showcased his sexy ass, with a white button-up cotton shirt that was rolled up at the sleeves, giving her an eyeful of his well-toned forearms — another one of her favorite things about him. She'd never seen him so casual, so relaxed-looking. Even the scowl that had been on his face earlier was gone.

She couldn't help the smile that spread on her lips.

He smiled back at her. Warm. Genuine.

It gave her hope and a butterfly flutter in her stomach.

"Another wine, miss?" the waiter asked.

"Yes, and one for me too," Trent said as he took a seat across from her. "Sorry I'm late."

She nodded.

"Have you ordered yet? I'm starving."

She watched him with curiosity as he picked up the menu, flicking his eyes across and down the page.

So he was going to keep her waiting. *Okay.* She could play that game too. Patience was definitely one of her strengths.

The waiter came back with their wine. "Are you ready to order?"

"Are you buying?" Trent popped those dimples at her, his eyes sparkling.

She laughed. "Yes, it's on me."

"Then I'll have the lobster."

"Make that two," she added.

The waiter smiled, picked up their menus and left them alone again. Even though they were seated off to the side, there wasn't much privacy to be had. The restaurant itself was nearly empty though, with only two other tables occupied.

"I was reading the files you gave me," he said after taking a drink of his wine.

Sabine nodded. The files she'd given him put her at a disadvantage and if Adam knew she'd passed them along to an outsider, he'd flip.

"Obviously I already knew that Harold was using your...um...services." Trent cleared his throat. "That Roy was making all the arrangements was startling."

She could tell it had more than startled him. He'd been shocked, was probably still shocked.

Roy not only made arrangements, he'd hand-selected some of the escorts that Harold had seen. Sabine hadn't known while it was happening. It had taken Adam's great investigation skills to dig that out. Roy wasn't stupid. He'd attempted to cover his trail, using a third party to make the arrangements. But why? Harold didn't need someone organizing that for him. He might have been a shady guy where his marriage was concerned, but he wasn't stupid. So what was the deal with Roy's involvement? That was the real question.

"And Harold's wife knew?" Trent shook his head.

"I'm not in this business to hurt women, and if I can avoid that collateral damage, I will. Harold's wife knew. I found out, just as you probably saw, that Roy was compensating her for the betrayal."

Trent nodded. "The women you employ...." He changed the subject, obviously feeling uncomfortable with the conversation.

He wasn't ready to deal with the information about Roy. That was fine.

"I shared the financial statements. You saw for yourself that they're not only fairly compensated but that they also have educational options available and job training for future planning. I take care of my girls, just as I take care of the people who are important to me."

"And Dylan Miller?" Trent asked, clearing his throat again.

Because that's what this is really about.

"Dylan was a very dear friend to me." Her voice caught. "I grew up with him. He's older than me, so of course he had an influence on me in a lot of ways. We were spoiled together, indulged like a little princess and prince. My father... He didn't like to discipline and I took advantage of that." She smiled wistfully. Her dad had been a wonderful man but avoided giving her any punishments. Looking back on it, Sabine could say that it was both a blessing and a curse. She'd had the freedom to be whoever she wanted to be, to explore any and all whims she'd thought up. That meant that she'd also had little guidance, no one, except maybe the media, to let her know when she'd overstepped boundaries. And she really did get a thrill from overstepping and all the attention it got her. "Anyway, I'm sure I know what Roy told you — that I chased his son all over the world, taking him from worthwhile pursuits and corrupting him."

"He did say that. He also said that you gave him the drugs that led to his overdose. That Adam was supplying him."

"Adam was using with him, supplying the both of them. That much is true. But I had no idea. I was building an empire at that point, very distracted with adulting. I'd cleaned up, was mired in paperwork and contracts and was sorting out my future. When I found out that Dylan was using, I tried to help. I got Adam clean, but Dylan? He refused. Adam and Dylan were close. *Very* close. And that was what was more revolting to Roy than anything else, I'll tell you. When Roy found out that Dylan was bi, that he was having a relationship with my right-hand man, a man who *he'd* hired as security for his son. Well, that was the last straw. He threatened to disown Dylan and was all set to disinherit him, then send him to a gay camp, to straighten him out. You know, one of those awful places that try to undo homosexuality by whatever means possible? Dylan was terrified and crushed that his father would do that to him. That's why Dylan overdosed. It had nothing to do with me."

Trent didn't speak. She could tell that he didn't know what to say.

"I don't have evidence to prove that." She let an edge tint her words. "But I can assure you that Adam tells a vivid version of Dylan's last call to him." Tears bubbled to her eyes, the memory of Adam weeping as he'd told her what Dylan had done. "Roy keeps him in that medical facility rotting away, forgotten until this moment, when he needed to show you how despicable I am. His father has power of attorney. Even though I tried to get Dylan some actual help, I have no legal grounds to do that. He's not being mistreated there, at least. He has the best care that money can buy."

And she made sure that stayed true, exerting her influence in ways that ensured the facility Dylan was at only hired the best care workers and had the best of the best of everything else.

Their food arrived. Silence fell. Sabine felt surprisingly hungry all of a sudden, like unburdening herself of those hard truths had freed her of the stress she was carrying. She'd told her version. Now it was up to Trent to decide which story he wanted to believe.

She dug in, cracking the lobster's shell, pulling the meat out. It smelled wonderful. It tasted even better.

"A few months ago, before Harold died, Ellie, my secretary, got an email." Trent let out a long breath, then picked up his shell cracker and got to work on his lobster. "She was confused and sent it to me. It was a financial statement that didn't fit with any of the ones she'd worked on for Morgan and Miller." *Crack.* "She thought I'd opened a separate account for one of the projects I was working on."

Sabine stopped chewing. What was he telling her?

Trent wasn't looking at her, though. He was focused on the food in front of him. "She didn't realize — and neither did I at the time — that it was an offshore account sent to Ellie in error." He chuckled but it sounded rough, tired. When he finally looked up at her, his eyes held a hard edge. "He's siphoning money from the company. Ellie didn't clue in to that, and I didn't want to burden her with the knowledge. Hell, I didn't really want the burden either so I buried it. I told her it was a mistake, not to worry about it."

"Are you serious?"

Trent nodded, his expression solemn.

Sabine picked up her phone. She needed to tell Adam.

"Don't," Trent said, his hand up. "Please, don't, not yet." He put his fork down. "Hours after that email was sent, our systems went down. It was so weird. The entire network collapsed. Our email was compromised by a hacker, IT said. They needed my computer, Ellie's too."

"They wiped them, right?" Sabine put her phone down again.

"Yeah, we lost everything. Even our email accounts were wiped," Trent said.

"So you have no way to prove it."

"I didn't say that," Trent said, looking down at his plate, his throat working as he gulped a couple of times.

"What?"

He looked up at her, his eyes blazing. "I printed the email, along with the statement."

"Where did you put it?"

He winced. "I asked Ellie to go pick it up from my place and courier it to me express. It should be here by the morning. I need to tell her to hold off." He dug his phone out of his pocket.

"No, hang tight on that. I can get us back to New York by the afternoon. Let her send the file." She rubbed her hands together. "Do you know what the media will do with this?" Sabine didn't even try to keep the glee out other voice. Trent couldn't blame her. This was just the kind of thing she needed to bury Roy.

"Yeah, I do." Trent sighed.

"He's using you, Trent, as a distraction, and I'm a pawn as well." That hurt her to say, but she saw it so clearly now. If Roy could stir up enough controversy with her and her company, it would deflect whatever grand plans he had connected to his offshore account. Maybe he was planning on draining the Morgan and Miller coffers once and for all, then taking off to some third-world country where the booze flowed and the authorities could be bought off. Maybe Harold had been in on it? Or maybe he wasn't as with it as Sabine had thought. Maybe he was easily distracted by the girls and let his job duty fall to Roy somehow.

"It's a lot to take in." Trent picked up a roll but didn't eat it. He just kind of held it, looking dejected. Sad.

She reached across the table to touch his hand. "Let me share this with Adam. He'll be able to sort out what needs to be done." She squeezed his fingers. "Please... It's time for Roy to pay for everything and stop him from destroying anyone else's life."

"Okay." Trent nodded. "But I do want to call Ellie and give her a heads up."

Sabine had picked up her phone. "Not yet, okay? You'll see her tomorrow, right after we land. I just don't want any possibility that Roy will find out you have those documents. She'll be safe. I promise. And you've told me a million times how discreet she is, how trustworthy."

Trent sucked in a deep breath, then nodded. "Okay, yeah... Ellie won't even peek in that file."

"Trust me, Trent. I've got this, and I won't let anything happen to you or the people you care about." She put the phone to her ear. "Adam, I've got something for you." She held the phone out to Trent.

He looked at her, then at the phone, sighed again, and took it from her. "Hey, Adam... Yeah, it's Trent. Listen..."

Chapter Fifteen

"Sex on a plane? Is that really a thing?" Trent teased Sabine as he followed her up the staircase from the tarmac. The sway of her hips had his dick pulsing. "Like the mile-high club?"

Sabine snickered. "Something like that—except we don't have to do it in a cramped washroom."

Trent hadn't spent the night with Sabine—but not because he didn't want to. He'd gone home after they'd finished dinner so he could spend some time with his parents and warn them, without scaring them, about what was going to happen. He and Sabine had a plan. Maybe it was a bit too big of a plan, but they had one, and when all was said and done, Trent would likely be in the news again. He'd wanted his parents to know what was happening, without really telling them what was going on. It had been tricky, to say the least.

Adam had sent the Kitty Calls private jet to Colorado to pick them up the next morning. It was on the way back after a quick stop to get one of the Kitty

Cats from a private engagement she'd been working over the last week. And true to her word, Ellie had sent the file express delivery. He'd had it in hand by eleven.

"Mistress," a tall, lithe redhead gushed as she greeted Sabine at the door. "I haven't seen you in ages!"

Mistress? Trent's cock perked to complete attention, nearly standing straight, his pants tenting noticeably.

Sabine curled her arm around the girl's neck, tangling her fingers in her long curls. "Lexi." She pulled the redhead closer and ran her closed lips along the girl's jaw.

Lexi seemed to melt at Sabine's touch, her body going languid.

Sabine released the girl, letting her slide to the carpeted floor. "Trent, this is Lexi. She's a very bad girl most of the time. I suspect she needs to be punished." Her eyes sparkled with mischief, a question there, waiting for an answer.

Was he interested?

This was a new development, not that he should be surprised. Sabine had never made a fuss about who she had been photographed kissing over the years. Some of her earliest recorded relationships had been with women. At the time, the media hadn't known what to do with that. Trent had spent many a night fantasizing about it though, jerking off to the idea of Sabine Cowan in a pile of tits and ass—and now here it was being offered to him.

He licked his lips. Lexi was looking up at him expectantly. Her pert little tits were encased in her form-fitting dress. He could imagine that they stood at attention when set free, perky and begging for a tongue. She appeared to be panting, her lips glistening, her hands on her knees. Sabine still had her fingers twisted in Lexi's hair.

"Lexi, do you want to deep throat Trent?" Sabine purred.

Trent's cock pulsed, straining against his zipper.

Lexi nodded eagerly. "Yes, Mistress."

Trent lifted his eyes to meet Sabine's. "This is okay with you?"

"Why wouldn't it be?" She leaned into him, her breasts brushing his arm as she kissed him tenderly. "I care about you, Trent. I want you in my life, and part of my life is exploring with other people. I like sex and you like sex. We shouldn't deny ourselves this pleasure. And trust me, Lexi is an absolute pleasure. The real question is, are *you* okay with that?"

Was he okay with that? It meant sharing her. "I want to be with you." But being with other people didn't mean they weren't together.

"Always," Sabine said, dropping her hand to his zipper. "So let's explore this together."

Trent nodded, his breath catching when his dick hit the open air. Lexi was on him in a heartbeat. Her warm mouth encased his tip first, coating him with saliva, pressing her tongue hard against his shaft. Sabine still had Lexi's hair in her grip, moving her slowly forward, then tugging her back so that Trent's aching cock popped from her lips.

"Let's move this to the bedroom. The plane will take off soon." Sabine didn't wait for a response. She just pulled Lexi to her feet and walked her out of the room, leaving Trent feeling slightly bewildered as he trailed behind, his cock aching for Lexi's mouth.

The engines were roaring alive as Trent stepped into the back room. It was more spacious than he'd expected. The jet itself wasn't huge, but the room had a king-size bed, with a closet to one side and a dresser on the other.

Sabine was standing by the dresser, opening drawers as she pulled out various things — whips and restraints.

Trent felt a rush of excitement amping up his already almost-painful arousal. Lexi was on the bed. She'd already slipped her dress off. Trent tripped on it as he shuffled into the room.

"Turn around," Sabine ordered.

For a split second, Trent thought she was ordering him, but Lexi shifted, her head down, eyes flickering up, gazing at him through her lashes. It was hot as fuck. Her black lace bra didn't leave much to the imagination, not that he minded. Her little pink nipples were pebbled, straining against the lace. Her panties had been pulled up at the middle, the cloth parting her pussy lips.

Sabine came over with leather restraints. "Put these on her." She handed them to Trent.

He licked his lips then took the restraints before latching them to Lexi's wrists behind her back. He tightened the buckles so that Lexi's shoulders drew back and her tits jutted out.

Sabine motioned for him to get on the bed. Lexi leaned down, ass in the air. He dropped his pants and slipped them off, along with his shoes, then pulled his shirt over his head. He climbed onto the mattress on his knees and nudged Lexi's mouth with his dick.

Trent's cock jolted as Lexi moaned, opening her mouth to take him in.

"All the way, Lexi," Sabine cooed.

Sabine stood beside the bed, a wicked smile curling her lips, watching as Lexi slipped her mouth over the head of his dick, down the shaft until he could feel the resistance of the back of her throat.

"Do you like his big dick, Lexi?" Sabine asked.

Lexi moaned again. The vibration of sound carried all the way up Trent's cock so that his balls felt it like a caress.

Sabine was still fully clothed, wearing a pink sundress, her breasts encased in a tight-fitting halter that pushed her cleavage up on display. She'd kicked her heels off as she turned to grab a small whip from the dresser. Trent would have giggled at the look she presented if it weren't so damn hot. Like a fifties housewife with her flower-print, flared-out dress that swished as she moved, her hair in a ponytail sliding over her shoulders, she lifted the whip and held it out to him. "Whip her."

He didn't think too hard on it. He just took the whip and did as Sabine had said. He raised the whip and slapped it against the top of Lexi's ass.

Lexi cried out, pulling her mouth back as she did. But Trent wouldn't let her move too far. Gripping her hair just as Sabine had, he pushed Lexi forward, encouraging her to take him all in once again.

"You're such a good girl, Lexi," Sabine said. "You always want to please me, don't you?"

Lexi tried to nod. Trent loosened his grip and directed Lexi's head back and forth so that she stroked him with her mouth and throat. Trent felt the rise of his climax and forced it back with all of his power. He wouldn't rush this...couldn't spew his load prematurely. No, he needed to ride this out for as long as he could. It was just too perfect.

"She has such cute little tits, doesn't she?"

Trent could only nod, all of his concentration focused on not blowing his cum down Lexi's throat.

Sabine smiled knowingly, an evil little smile that Trent knew very well.

"Do you want to watch me fuck myself while she's sucking you off?" Sabine asked.

Lexi made a small mewing noise, her mouth moving rhythmically up and down his shaft.

What? Trent's brain nearly exploded.

"You want me to pleasure myself, big boy?"

Yes. Fuck. Yes. Trent nodded, licking his lips and concentrating so hard that his whole body felt like it was going to burst.

Sabine moved to the dresser again, while at the same time unzipping the back of her dress. It fell to the floor, revealing that she was completely naked — no panties, no bra. Why that always shocked him, he would never understand.

Trent's cock pulsed hard. He felt the urge to come, his balls tightening, his eyes watering. *Ah fuck... Fuck...*

Sabine grabbed a vibrant blue dildo. It bobbed as she moved, looking both sexy and silly at the same time, effectively tempering his need to come, curiosity distracting him enough to pull him back from the edge.

Lexi was making a sucking noise as she drew back then forward, creating a vacuum in her mouth that made his cock feel so fucking good.

Sabine climbed onto the bed and positioned herself so that so that her pussy was on display.

Trent set the whip aside then tightened his grip on Lexi's hair with one hand. With the other, he reached forward to tease Sabine's nipple, the hard peak begging for a lick. She threw her head back as he played, flicking, pinching. When she brought her head back down and locked eyes with him, he felt the pulse of his orgasm rise swiftly once again. With one fluid motion, Sabine stuffed herself to the hilt, encasing the dildo in her pussy.

Trent pumped his hips and Sabine pumped hers. They worked in a rhythm, where Lexi rocked on Trent's dick and Sabine rocked her own pussy. Trent managed to hold on for a few minutes, but then Sabine reached her hand down and played with her clit.

That was too much for Trent to handle. His orgasm crashed in a blinding wave of pleasure so intense that he thought it would never end. His moan sounded more like a roar, just a bellow of noise that rocked his whole body, along with his never-ending stream of cum. And Lexi took it all, every last spasm, every last drop. She sucked him hard, keeping him deeply seated in her throat.

Sabine worked her clit and pumped her pussy until she was writhing and vibrating, moaning her own release.

Sabine smiled at him as she pulled the dildo out. It was coated in her cream. Much to his surprise, his own cock responded to the sight of that, hardening back to the point of intense aching once again.

"Lexi," Sabine said, her eyes still locked on Trent's.

Lexi pulled herself up, her chest heaving and lips glistening as she waited for the next instruction.

"Untie her hands," Sabine ordered.

Trent moved forward, his fingers clumsy as he worked to unlatch Lexi's bonds. His dick pressed against her ass cheek, his tip wet with cum, gliding over her smooth flesh.

Sabine slipped her hand under the sheet and pulled out a row of condoms. "You wanna fuck her, big boy?" Lexi pushed her ass back, letting his cock tease at her hole, an offering.

Sabine threw the condoms toward him. It was both a command and a question.

Trent wanted to. He wanted to slide his dick into that slick little hole of Lexi's. He flicked his gaze from Sabine's eyes to her pussy, watching with fascination as Sabine moved her fingers back to her lips.

Sabine had a lazy, satisfied smile on her face. "I want you to fuck her, Trent. I want her to feel your huge cock."

Trent picked up the condoms and opened a package, slipping one on quickly, his cock really weeping now.

"You're sure?" he asked as he positioned himself against Lexi's hot little cunt. This wasn't cheating. Even if he was lusting for this sweet girl in front of him, he was also lusting for Sabine — and she wanted him to do this.

"I want to watch you fuck her. I'm dying to see you pound her tight little pussy." And for a moment, Sabine threw her head back, lost as she slipped her own fingers deep into herself.

Trent watched her writhe, her glorious body moving as she pumped her sweet cunt. He loved the wanton abandon she showed as her skin flushed and her smile grew.

He needed to fuck Lexi so Sabine could watch.

Trent slid his cock in, the stretch of Lexi's pussy squeezing his shaft tightly, making him moan so loudly that Sabine opened her eyes again, a wicked smile on her lips.

"She's good, right? Tight, wet, hot."

Trent nodded. "Really fucking good. Really fucking tight." He rolled his hips, pumping her slowly, easing his girth into her body.

Lexi moaned, pushing back into him so that his balls smacked her flesh with force, encouraging him to go harder, faster, deeper. He reached around to play with her little tits. His hands covered them completely when he cupped her. He pulled her wispy bra down so he could flick her pebbled nipples.

Sabine was playing with her own — cupping, flicking, pinching. Her skin was pink, a sheen of sweat covering her flesh, her hips rising as she arched her back.

Trent's cock pulsed — the sensation of gliding in and out of Lexi while watching Sabine finger fuck herself was just too much sensation.

He knew the moment Sabine's orgasm started to crest. She pumped her fingers more frantically. Her moans sounded urgent, and Trent just kept on slamming Lexi with brutal thrust after thrust, feeling like his cock was pushing through resistance each time, her little sheath accommodating him somehow.

Sabine cried out as her orgasm rolled over her and Trent's own climax rose again, making him take hold of Lexi's hips so he could ram her harder, thrust deeper, until he came with a bellowing roar.

Chapter Sixteen

Sabine drew little circles with her finger along Lexi's soft skin. She had the delicious swells and curves that Sabine loved, but she also had definition and tone that made her body powerful.

"How's the training going?" Sabine asked.

Lexi lifted her arm up to cradle her head, sighing as she nestled a little closer into Sabine. "Really good. I've got a competition next month."

Lexi was a gymnast and she trained hard. When she'd come into Sabine's world, it had been because she was looking for adventure and excitement. The world of competitive sport wasn't doing it for her like it had and she'd wanted to explore a darker side of herself. Like all the girls who worked for Sabine, Lexi had been taken through a four-week training course, learning the ins and outs of Kitty Calls, with classes ranging from asserting dominance and setting boundaries, to double penetration and sucking cock. Sabine set all her girls up with a bank account and sat down with each of them to plan out a pathway to success. After all, bodies didn't stay young forever and the girls needed a way to be independent when they decided to leave the company. They were vetted extensively too, of course. Their entire life history was laid out, with their permission, so that Sabine and Adam could be sure of their loyalty and discretion.

"Did you have a good weekend with the senator?" Sabine continued to trace Lexi's skin tenderly. Although they'd been sexually intimate in the past—and perhaps would be again—right now she was only interested making sure Lexi felt loved and cherished.

Lexi giggled. "Oh yes, I did. I uploaded my notes to the database." She turned toward Sabine, her green eyes sparkling. "He sure does like to talk a lot about work."

"Yes, he does. Good girl," Sabine said, then moved closer so she could kiss Lexi's cheek.

Working for Kitty Calls meant information exchange. Her girls were trained in coaxing secrets from their clients, to listen carefully and to remember details. Sabine had access to a lot of information, all filed away in her secure database. She never did know when those things would come in handy.

"Harold McKibbon... He was one of yours too, right?" Sabine rolled away from Lexi, nestling closer to Trent, her hand straying over his abs.

Adam had been hunting through all of Morgan and Miller's CFO's files. The man hadn't talked as much as she would have expected, but he'd talked to some extent, and he'd preferred Lexi to most of the other girls on the roster who enjoyed fucking fat executives. He wasn't rough or mean with the girls, but he did have a healthy sexual appetite. When he needed a boost, he had a prescription to help him out.

"Oh yes, he liked to pour whiskey on my pussy and suck it off. It was fun. He always made sure I came."

Sabine leaned down and licked Trent's nipple. "Hmm, that sounds like a great idea." She rolled her tongue along the beaded pebble, nipping gently, her other hand roaming down Trent's flat stomach to his rising dick. She could pour some whiskey there and suck it off.

"I'm sorry he died. He wasn't a bad man." Lexi paused. "He hated his partner, that Roy asshole." She slid out of bed.

"Roy was using Kitty Calls to distract Harold." Sabine chuckled a bit that Trent was so dead asleep that he didn't even feel her roving hands. She turned to face Lexi, crooking her arm again, resting her head on her hand. "You were with him the night before he died. I was reading your notes last night. You mentioned that Roy popped by the condo."

One of the conditions of regular client services was that the client rented a space—condo, loft, apartment, whatever—for their time with the girls. It couldn't be a hotel, not when there were going to be ongoing appointments. Harold had gone one step further and had bought a condo in the Upper East Side, telling his wife that it was there for the many nights he needed to stay in the city.

His wife, of course, had known better. But she hadn't cared. She'd had her own side entertainment going on while her husband spent his time with his Kitty Cats.

Lexi started picking up her clothes. "Yeah, Roy was there. I didn't see him, just heard him at the door. He sounded a little annoyed, which wasn't surprising. The way Harold talked about him, he had a major pickle up his ass about everything."

"Well, that's true," Sabine laughed. "What was he there for? Did Harold say?"

"He brought Harold a prescription he'd left at the office or something. I think it was probably his blue pills." Lexi laughed. "He liked to fuck all night, that one...but his body just wouldn't do it for him sometimes unless he took a pill."

"Yes, that's what you said in your notes."

Harold was a big guy, probably pushing at least a hundred pounds overweight. He liked his booze and his food, but he liked the girls more. When he wasn't with Lexi, which was at least three times a month, he was with some of the other girls. So he was a busy guy, definitely the kind of person to indulge all his appetites. No one was surprised that he'd died in his sleep. It had probably been a heart attack, if Sabine was going to put money on it.

"Were you recording that night, by chance?" Sabine asked.

Lexi didn't answer right away, but her slow nod told Sabine what she wanted to hear. "Actually, yeah I was. Not live stream, of course—I don't do that with clients—but I did record our session. Harold liked to watch the highlights. He'd paid for the premium package."

"You think you could take some time and hunt that night down for me?"

Sabine had been meaning to follow up with Lexi for weeks now. She'd been curious about Harold's death and what had come before he'd died. Of course, Lexi hadn't ever been in danger of being caught up in an investigation, mainly because there hadn't been one. Harold McKibbon was found dead in his bed by his housekeeper. The preliminary police report, which Sabine had read, said that there was no sign of struggle. For all intents and purposes, the big guy had died a peaceful death. There was no trace of Lexi, no connection to Kitty Calls.

After reading Lexi's notes, Sabine had been more than curious about why Roy was really there. The dropping off of pills seemed like a job better suited to a secretary. So why had Roy made the delivery himself?

"Hell yes, I can." Lexi smiled. "Anything for you, Mistress."

"You're a good girl," Sabine said. "We'll be landing soon. Time to wake up Trent."

"You like him, huh?" Lexi turned toward the door.

Sabine pushed herself up to sit. "Yeah, there's something about him."

"He's open," Lexi said. "Totally open. He can't hide anything from you. That's what you like about him, I bet. It's probably super refreshing, right? To find a man who isn't hiding shit from you? Who doesn't have an ulterior motive? He's like Adam that way, someone you can trust..."

Sabine smiled. Yes, exactly like Adam that way...and yet different. There were very few people she could let her guard down with. Lexi was one, so was Adam and now Trent too, and there was so much more for them to explore together.

"I'm going to wake him up Kitty style," Sabine said.

Lexi nodded knowingly and opened the door. "I'll get to work on finding what you need."

Sabine shimmied down Trent's body, still marveling that he was asleep. Maybe Lexi had worn him out.

Sabine had always loved sharing in her relationships. She'd known that pushing Trent this way could backfire. He was a one-woman kind of guy—at least on the surface of things. Helping him understand that sex was sex and love was love—two sometimes separate things—was important to her. But Trent hadn't rejected the idea. It helped, of course, that Lexi was so fucking sexy, her body responding enthusiastically to every touch, every stroke.

"Mm-m," Sabine groaned as she slipped Trent's dick into her mouth.

Trent groaned too, and he cracked his eyes open. "Oh...hello there."

Sabine smiled around his dick.

Lexi slipped out of the room quietly, the light click of the door closing letting Sabine know that they were alone.

Sabine shifted so she could straddle Trent, rubbing her pussy ever so gently along the shaft of his cock.

He lifted his hands to reach for her. She leaned down toward him so he could cup her breasts.

"Trent, you wanna have a little fun with me?" Sabine asked, her voice singsong as she continued to rub her pussy along his shaft. "I'm feeling like getting fucked—double fucked right now." She reached over and grabbed a dildo and some lube.

His eyes were wide open now, his dick hard once again. "Oh yeah." Then he saw what she was doing and he let a slow smile spread on his lips. "Oh hell yeah!"

Sabine swatted his hands from her tits and spun herself around, lifting her ass in the air so that she could spear herself with the dildo. They both let out a collective groan as the dildo slipped inside Sabine's pussy. She pulled it back out, then pumped herself a few times more before wedging it back in deep. She'd picked a mid-sized dildo, stretching herself out in just the right way. It would be a tight fit with Trent's cock too, but she really wanted him to stuff her ass while she fucked her own pussy.

"Ready, big boy?" She turned to Trent, leaning down so she could wrap her lips around his cock, her ass in his face. He nuzzled his mouth between her cheeks, licking her asshole briefly, making her moan.

She popped her mouth off his dick then covered his shaft with some lube.

Trent pushed back and moved up to his knees, his hands on Sabine's thighs, thumbs parting her ass cheeks once again. Looking over her shoulder, she watched him run his finger along his shaft, collecting lube before rubbing her asshole, massaging his way inside so he could stretch her out. She shivered, enjoying the sensual probing. After slipping another finger in and pumping her a few times, he finally pulled out and positioned himself for the real deal.

Sabine nudged back so his dick was prodding her hole. His cock was big, but she could take him and the dildo. She wanted to feel stuffed full. Her tits swayed, her nipples ached — so many sensations all at once.

Pulses of pleasure zapped her brain as Trent eased his cock into her. The feeling of being full of two unyielding forces at the same time made her jolt, take a deep breath and pant her way through as he moved slowly into her ass. She moaned again, a long, low sound that rumbled through her body. Trent could barely fit to the hilt, but once he was in, he stopped moving for a second or two, giving her time to adjust, to let the sensations roll through her. It was so much...not too much...just a lot. Sabine sucked in a deep breath then let it out. She bucked her hips and Trent slid his cock back, then he slammed himself in, hard, fast, pumping her while she reached down to stroke her clit.

The sensation of her rubbing her fingers in all the right places, the dildo moving counter to Trent's cock and her body swaying and shuddering, was all consuming. Her brain was misfiring, ramped up on adrenaline and lust, jolts of pleasure that were so intense Sabine couldn't stop moaning. Her orgasm didn't build slowly. It ramped up with each of Trent's thrusts, making her shudder, her body spasming, her climax spilling through her like a wave of pleasure that pinged her every nerve ending. She screamed her release and Trent came right after her, pumping her ass full of his cum, hot jets soaking into her again and again.

This was the secret side of her life. The intensity of sharing herself with Trent was more intoxicating than any other aspect of her world. It was addictive, it was overwhelming and all she could do was ride it out until every last pulse roared through her.

Chapter Seventeen

Trent had to suspend a lot of his hard-wired beliefs about how things would go in his life, his ideas about success and what exactly loyalty meant. His understanding of people and how they were motivated, which differed in many ways from his own beliefs, had to shift. The way he'd understood things before was different from the way he understood them now and that was hard to reconcile.

His parents hadn't prepared him for hard life decisions like this. *Don't do drugs. Don't gamble. Don't spend what you don't have. Work hard.* They'd raised him to be a good person, to consider the other guy and to take no shit, not to be a pushover but also to do no harm. He'd been okay with that. It had worked for him. He'd kept his head down and worked his ass off. He'd accomplished things. Life was good.

But he could see how that kind of thinking was also really naïve. Because in reality, the other guy wasn't always going to treat people fairly and it was stupid to believe that other people would avoid doing harm. Sometimes it was every man for himself.

He could say that it was all Sabine's fault, place blame on her influence in his life. Because before Sabine, life had been a lot less complicated. But that would be an asshole thing to do. She wasn't the problem. Her appearance in his life hadn't been the catalyst for what was happening now. His naïveté had put him there—that and putting his faith in Roy Miller.

Trent's thoughts were heavy with all of these things. So heavy that sitting in his office for probably the last time—no, definitely the last time—was proving to be more difficult than he'd anticipated, especially since he was currently running a program on his computer that was siphoning information for Sabine. And yes, Trent realized he was acting like one of Sabine's Kitty Cats, who, as he'd come to understand, acted as spies as well as escorts.

He wasn't sure how he felt about that, other than knowing in his gut that, even though it was the hard thing to do, it was also the right thing to do. Adam had suspicions that revolved around the financial statement that had been sent to Ellie in error. It had been a fluke that he had never been meant to see but had.

"Definitely an offshore account," Adam informed Trent when they sat down the day before to hash out the details about what he'd discovered.

"Like a tax haven?" Trent was trying not to notice how Sabine sat next to Adam and not him. He was trying to avoid crossing the distance and snatching her hand. There was no room for this shit in their relationship, though, so, while the impulse was strong, his control was stronger.

She'd opened up part of her life to him that he had never experienced and hadn't even realized he was capable of. Being intimate with another woman while Sabine had watched had rocked his world, but it had also confirmed what he had been suspecting for a while. He truly did love Sabine and that meant loving her with all the perks and baggage that came along with her lifestyle.

One man, one woman... That was what his parents had modeled for him. That was how he'd come to understand relationships. But that wasn't how Sabine embraced her relationships. She wasn't jealous, even though he'd come inside another woman. She wasn't checking her insecurities against his interests. She'd given him something the other day — a piece of her life that Trent was certain not many people had a chance to experience.

"Tax haven for ill-gotten funds, yeah." Adam's muscles flexed as he turned his laptop toward Trent.

Trent tried not to notice how fluid his movements were or how much bulkier he was compared to Trent's own body. Check those insecurities, bud, he silently chided, resisting the urge to flex his own muscles.

Nope... This was not going to be an issue for Trent, not anymore.

"I believe that Roy is moving money around so that he can skim off the top and funnel it into this account. I also believe, based on what I have been seeing in our own accounts, that he's using Kitty Calls to hide the transfers."

That startled Trent. "He's doing what?"

"I don't have proof...yet...but I think that Roy is somehow moving the cash in a way that makes it look like it's going to entertainment, also known as Harold McKibbon's Kitty Calls services, but in actuality, that's just the tip of the iceberg. He's moving more substantial funds to this offshore account."

"That's hard to swallow," Trent blurted.

Sabine reached out and entwined her fingers with his. "I know it seems farfetched, but you've got a piece of the puzzle right here." She nodded to the red file folder marked 'Backups'. "And you saw the truth in the files I shared with you. Roy isn't the man you thought he was. I know that's hard – "

"It's not that," Trent interrupted, giving her hand a bit of squeeze. "Yes, he was my mentor and I looked up to him. Yes, this is all very surreal, because I thought... Well, I thought the man was infallible, which is stupid really." He sighed. "It just seems too direct a path, too easy to trace it to Roy. He might be a corrupt man, but he's not a stupid one."

"Yeah, that's for sure." Adam turned the computer back so he could type. For such a big guy, his fingers were flying. "The program I created sussed this out of our records after six hours of searching. Our links are weak and our evidence weaker. But there are patterns that are more than just coincidences. Roy organized some of the bank transfers to coincide with the Kitty Call visits. I cross-referenced the dates and they match up. So there was the distraction factor, for sure, to keep Harold preoccupied with the girls so that he wouldn't notice what Roy was up to. But there's also this..." He turned the computer toward Trent once again. "Take a look."

Trent leaned forward and watched the video cued on the screen. "Is that – ?"

"Yeah, it is. Check the time," Adam said.

"The coroner's report said that Harold died in the early morning hours...roughly around three," Sabine added.

"Ah, shit." Trent's shoulders slumped. His whole body deflated. He watched the video scroll through the time. "Could there be any other explanation?"

"The housekeeper shows up about two hours after she leaves," Sabine said. "Then the paramedics arrive."

Trent sucked in a deep breath then let it out. Every truth he'd thought he knew unraveled right before his eyes.

He knew what he had to do. The right thing wasn't always the easy thing.

And Adam had provided him with the means necessary to do the hard thing, to choose his loyalty.

By the countdown timer on the lower left of his screen, Trent had five minutes left before the program got everything it needed. Then they'd be able to make some decisions on where to go with this. Embezzlement was one thing but murder was a whole other monster.

Trent pushed his coffee aside. He was jittery enough as it was. His whole world was about to shift on its axis once again, but this time he was the one orchestrating it. Having power and control over the situation only changed it a little. He wasn't totally surprised by the guilt he was feeling. He just wanted to get the hell out of there once and for all.

Trent started tapping his fingers on his desk, growing more and more anxious. He hadn't run into anyone in the building, but only because he'd arrived hours before anyone would be there. And that was how he'd wanted it. Get in and get out.

Three minutes.

He scanned his office. *Fuck.* He loved this space, all the dark wood and the leather. His gaze settled on the couch where he and Sabine had fucked — and the chair, the floor, the wall... She was imprinted all over the place. He smiled. Well, at least the ghost of their exploits would be left behind when he finally got his ass out of there. He turned his chair so he could look out of the window, squinting into the growing light. When he'd arrived, it'd been dark still. He'd left Sabine's bed reluctantly and made his way to his office before the building had actually opened. Adam's buddy, lobby security, had waved him in without much of a glance.

Now the sun was rising high, promising a hot day.

His computer beeped. Trent glanced to the ceiling and winked. *Finally!* He let out a breath and turned. He reached out to grab the USB, his fingers curled around its body, when his office door opened.

"Oh, Trent! I didn't know you'd be in today!" Ellie's face showed her shock, her eyes wide, an instant blush rising to her cheeks. She'd obviously just come in. Her purse was still on her shoulder and her sunglasses were perched on top of her head, trapping her hair back from her face.

Trent pulled the USB from his computer and slipped it into his pocket.

"I thought I heard a noise in here. I wasn't sure it was you, though." Ellie's gaze tracked his movements. "I'm going to let Roy know you're here. He wants to speak to you."

"I bet he does," Trent said as he stood, "but I'm leaving."

"What's going on, Trent?" Ellie moved into the office, closing the door behind her. "Did something happen between you and Roy?" The way she said it was too full of concern, too cloying in tone.

"Ellie, I don't want to do this with you." He moved around his desk. "I have to go."

She moved in front of the door, her tiny body barely blocking it. "I can't let you leave, not until I've called Roy."

Trent kept moving.

Ellie reached into her purse and pulled out a gun. It was small, just the right size to conceal in a little bag, but deadly-looking all the same.

"What the fuck, Ellie?" Trent stopped short, his hands up, his heart thudding.

"Give me whatever you have in your pocket, then you can leave."

"Ellie, are you crazy? You don't know how to use a gun! Where'd you even get that?"

Her expression hardened. "I *do* know how to use a gun, Trent. I have used a gun many times. You really don't know a thing about me. You never really bothered to get to know me, did you?" She motioned for him to back up. "Take a seat at your desk and make sure I can see your hands."

"Ellie, there's no need — "

"Stop talking and sit down. I need to call Roy so he knows you're here."

"Then what? You're going to shoot me?"

"I don't want to." Ellie's voice cracked a bit. "But I will if I have to." She motioned again. "Take a seat and empty your pockets on the desk. Slowly...please," she added.

He decided that it would be best not to get shot. He had no way of knowing how sensitive that trigger was, but he wasn't willing to take a chance. Ellie hadn't taken her finger off it since she'd brandished the gun, and that made him nervous as hell.

"Okay, I'll do as you say." He moved slowly backward until he was back at his chair. He maneuvered awkwardly until he was sitting.

"Now empty your pockets...*slowly*," she repeated. "Then put your hands on the desk so I can see them."

Trent did what she wanted, pulling the USB out and laying it on the desk.

"Hands flat."

He did that too. His palms were sweaty, his heart hammering.

Ellie moved to the desk, her actions brisk. She glanced at the USB but picked up the phone with her free hand. The gun was still pointed at his chest. He had the split-second thought of trying to snatch it from her, but knowing him, he'd be more likely to make it go off right in his face. *Better not to play the hero right now.*

"Good morning, Kelly. Yes, it looks like a lovely day. Oh sure, a walk at lunch would be wonderful. Is Roy in yet? Great! Could you let him know that Trent is here? Yes, in his office. Sure thing! See you then." She put the phone back down and moved to snatch the USB.

Trent stopped her with his hand over hers. "Ellie, don't."

She snapped the gun to his face, forcing him to literally stare down the barrel. "Don't touch me!"

He lifted his hand from hers, trying to keep the trembling from showing. "Ellie—"

"You don't know what it's like"—she didn't pull the gun back—"trying to get ahead in this business."

"This isn't the way, Ellie." Trent gulped. "I know what you've done."

She held his stare, no doubt assessing him as if they were thinking the same thing.

"No." She flinched.

"What were you thinking?" he asked her.

"What was *I* thinking?" She barked a laugh. "I was thinking that I'd never be able to pay off my dad's gambling debt. I was thinking that life wasn't fair and the good guy deserves to be screwed just like I've been—and all because my dad can't keep his vices under control. I was thinking that Harold McKibbon had it coming and that making him look corrupt is what he deserved after all of his affairs, all of his indulgences. The man was a pig."

"He had a wife...kids..."

"He didn't care about anyone but himself." Ellie's voice was cold again, the flare of emotion gone.

The video Adam had shown Trent was security footage of Ellie entering Harold's building, then his condo. The time stamp was two-thirty a.m. Then she'd left shortly after three, right around the time Harold was dying.

"I didn't kill him," she stated.

"Are you sure about that?"

"All his booze and drugs... The pills Roy brought him that night..." She trailed off, biting her lip.

Trent pieced the puzzle together, his gut clenching. "You knew what was going to happen. You knew Harold would die from those pills."

Tears sprang to Ellie's eyes. "I made sure he took them. That was my job. I had a key. He was expecting me to come clean up, to take care of the evidence. You know what it's like picking up after a man like that? After he's been with one of those filthy girls?" She spat those last words, her face distorting. "Yeah, I made sure he took his dose. Then I checked his pulse. I confirmed he was dead."

"You watched him die and left him there to be found by his housekeeper. Ellie..."

"Don't you dare judge me." She pulled the USB toward her. "I can't let you leave with this. If he goes down, so do I."

"It's only a matter of time, Ellie." Trent sighed.

"If I'd only been more careful... I didn't mean to send that email to you. It was so stupid...so careless."

"Was I always the scapegoat?" Trent asked, his voice sounding throaty, emotion threatening to clog his words. "When Roy sent me to meet Sabine, was it always the plan to throw me to the media?"

"Yes..." Ellie tried to be hard, her face taking on a self-righteous lift, an attempt to look down her nose at him, but her voice sounded rough, wobbly, like she was going to cry. "But I didn't think that you'd keep seeing her, Trent. I didn't mean for — "

"How?" he barked. "You paid for those photos, right? You leaked the video." His head was spinning as everything started falling in place. Harold's death followed by Trent's set-up... It had all been meant to pull the attention away from Roy.

Ellie flinched. "One of her girls, *a Kitty Cat*... She's family and she owed me a favor." She sneered. "It was supposed to be her and you. But then Ms. Cowan got her claws into you instead. It actually couldn't have worked out better. I leaked the photos and the video to get attention on you so we could..." She paused, waved her free hand around. "You know."

"Embezzle money?"

"It was all for the greater good!" Ellie's bravado wavered, and the hand holding the gun shook. "Roy and I... We did what we had to do. And we only need one more transfer, then we can leave. He'll take care of his family, his son, and I'll take care of my dad. Then we'll leave...and be together."

Trent flinched, pity making his stomach drop. "Oh, Ellie, is that what he told you? That what he was going to take you away?" Trent slammed his fist against the desk, making her flinch harder and take a step back. "He's using you just like he's using me. We're pawns, Ellie."

"No! *You're* the pawn, Trent. Not me." Her cruel smile returned, marring her features almost beyond recognition. She levelled the gun at him once again. "I *will* shoot you. I'll make it so that you can't tell anyone."

Trent shook his head. "I guess in the end, it really doesn't matter, because you're right. If Roy goes down, so do you."

Her resolve seemed to waver. "What do you mean?"

Trent motioned to his computer. The screen was black.

"What?" Ellie waved for him to move, so he hit the escape key on his computer.

The screen came to life, showing a live feed. Ellie — the gun in her hand, her expression crashing from disbelief to horror... He nodded over his shoulder toward the small camera he'd clipped to the drapes above the window. "I installed it myself. We were going to keep an eye on things here after I left."

Ellie's mouth gaped. The gun shook.

Trent raised his hands in the air and shifted back in his chair. "Your move, Ellie."

"This is all her doing, isn't it?" Ellie shrieked, her eyes wild. "Before that bitch got involved in your life, you would never have done this to me!"

"I haven't done anything to you, Ellie." He was trying to stay calm, but *fuck*, that gun could go off at any moment, and he wasn't entirely sure how this was all going to go down. "And neither has Sabine."

"Don't you say her name to me like that! Like she has done nothing wrong... Like she's so innocent... That low-life dirty whore has a thing or two coming her way as well." Ellie's finger twitched.

Trent closed his eyes, knowing that he'd never move fast enough to get out of the way of a bullet. He'd like to think his life was flashing before his eyes, but really, all he was thinking about was not pissing his pants out of fear.

"Drop the weapon! Drop the weapon right now!" SWAT burst through his office door and life as Trent knew it shifted out of balance forever.

Chapter Eighteen

Sabine was jittery — an unusual feeling for her, but one that was totally related to Trent and the sight of him facing a loaded weapon.

They'd agreed to install a camera in Trent's office as a way to surveil what was going on at Morgan and Miller after Trent had left for good. No one had expected that it would be the very thing that saved Trent's life.

His life! She hadn't expected the meek little secretary to come in brandishing a gun. She'd expected Roy to be all blustering and loud, to throw his weight around and make threats...but the secretary? Nowhere near Sabine's radar.

She'd watched in absolute horror as the woman had pulled a gun and threatened the man she loved with it. That was right. Trent, the man she loved. One she didn't want to lose — not to violence or to anything or anyone else.

Despite the fact that everything had gone down with no one getting hurt, Sabine was still on edge. She'd notified the police. They'd sent SWAT, the secretary had been arrested and Trent was on his way to her place after spending time giving statements at the police station. Adam was with him, which left Sabine alone to dwell on everything that had happened.

She wasn't drinking, even though wine would probably numb her a bit. She couldn't relax until Trent was safely there with her, so she was watching the security cameras, waiting for him and Adam to arrive, tapping her nails against the top of her desk and driving herself insane with anticipation.

Her feelings about everything seemed crystal clear now. Ellie had divulged a lot of information in her live-stream interview. She'd implicated Roy in some ways. Now, Sabine had to decide just what she would do with it all. Adam's buddy at Morgan and Miller would remove the camera. Trent himself had the USB with information that would also help incriminate Roy. How she would use it was the final decision and one that she'd be making with Trent and Adam.

She left out a sigh of relief when her car pulled into the parking entrance. They were back. *Finally.*

She was on her way to the door when Trent burst in, his frantic gaze landing on her immediately. He pounded toward her, catching her in his arms and lifting her, crushing her with a kiss that took her breath away. It was a hard, urgent, tongue-probing, mouth-claiming kiss.

"I literally saw my life flash before my eyes," he said after he pulled away, leaving her a little shell-shocked by his lips.

She laughed as she stumbled backward, not getting too far out of his grasp.

"Did you see her gun?" His eyes were wide, his voice excited.

Sabine nodded, emotion crashing through her. She reached up to cup his face. "I was scared for you. I-I-I thought I might lose you."

Trent held her stare for a moment, clearly reading her soul, a look of possessive urgency flashing back at her.

He let go of her hips, reached up and pulled her blouse apart, buttons bouncing off in all directions. She gasped, then moaned as he cupped her breasts, squeezing her through her bra, bringing his lips to her collar, then her neck, nipping and licking until she was melting.

She helped him take his shirt off, unbuttoning slowly as he continued to kiss her neck, her jaw, the tops of her breasts, still squeezing them and pushing her bra down so that her nipples popped out and he could kiss there too. She moaned as he used his thumbs to rub them against the edge of the bra, abrading her then soothing with his lips and tongue.

"Sabine, I—"

The door of the condo opened and Adam walked in. He froze, zeroing in on them, their half-dressed state and the flush on their faces.

He bit his bottom lip, his eyes hooded, and he moved his hand to his crotch. "I'll leave," he said gruffly.

"No, Adam, don't." Sabine lifted her hand, stopping him with a gesture before turning back to Trent. "Trent…we could invite Adam to join us."

Trent tensed, his hands frozen on her, uncertainty in his eyes.

She lifted her hands to cup his face and locked him into her gaze. "Trent, I love you. I want you. I'm pretty sure I want to spend the rest of my life with you, if you'll have me. But part of me comes with Adam and Lexi and others. Will you share my life and my body? Will you let Adam join us?"

Trent's gaze was flickering back and forth, his thoughts likely whirring.

"You're mine," Trent growled.

"My heart belongs, in part, to you, but my body belongs to me and I like to share it with many partners. I'd love for you to be okay with that, so we could share our passion with others, together."

She could see the hesitation in his eyes...the doubt. And if he ultimately wasn't okay with it then she would ask Adam to leave.

Trent opened his mouth...then closed it again. He looked toward Adam, who was still standing there, looking his usual gorgeous self, his hand cupping his cock, obviously ready to go.

Trent turned back to Sabine then gave a slight nod. "Okay," he croaked. "Yeah, okay."

Sabine felt a surge of glee. Beaming, she motioned to Adam. "Let's take this to my bedroom where we'll be comfortable."

She took Trent's hand, entwining her fingers with his, her heart pounding, excitement like a shiver over her body. He'd said yes. It was a fantasy come true. She led him to her king-size bed and encouraged him onto it with her.

She pulled her blouse off completely. "Adam, strip for us."

Adam took his position at the end of the bed, still standing on the floor. He pulled his phone out of his pocket and scrolled through the screen, landing on the music he knew she liked. When the sound blasted, he started his dance—one he was damn good at.

Sabine kept working, though, removing her clothes quickly—bra, pants, panties, socks—everything off in record time so that she could unbutton Trent's pants, unzip then pull out his gloriously stiff cock.

And he was rock-hard, even as he looked between her and Adam and lingered on Adam's muscles, how they flexed and moved, how fluid he was rolling his body to the music, taking his own pants off, holding his own erect cock in his hand. Trent only looked away for seconds, then he was looking back at Adam. And Sabine would admit, Adam was mesmerizing, but she'd seen the show before.

She nudged her mouth against Trent's cock, running the length of it along her cheek, feeling the soft skin and the wet precum weeping onto her flesh. She opened her mouth and took him in, bending over so that her ass was in the air.

Trent moaned.

Adam took the cue—gripping her ass in his hands, he shoved his face between her legs.

It was Sabine's turn to moan then, letting the vibration carry over Trent's head and along his shaft. His hands were in her hair, holding her tightly as she sucked and licked and stroked, trying to stay focused. Adam was good at eating ass though—really, really fucking good. He rubbed her asshole with his tongue, delving inside while he worked her pussy with his fingers, circling her clit with his strong thumb and hooking her G-spot. She was writhing in no time. She moved her mouth up and down on Trent's dick, her pussy weeping with Adam's attention and her ass lubed up and soaking. She just couldn't hang on for a moment longer.

Her orgasm crashed and crashed again as she squirted all over Adam's neck and chest, gushing while she pumped Trent's dick, coaxing him over the edge so he was coming deep into her throat, hot jets of fluid that she sucked.

He fucked her throat for a minute longer, his cock still really hard, even after he'd unloaded into her mouth.

"That was..." Trent dropped his head back, loosening his fingers in Sabine's hair. "Ah fuck...that was awesome!"

Sabine smiled, any concerns she might have, that Trent would change his mind or get cold feet, slipping away. He was smiling when he looked down at her, his eyes sparkling.

"You suck his dick now and I'll fuck you," Trent ordered.

Nope, no hesitation there.

She did as he'd commanded. She turned around and pulled Adam closer, moving him to the side of the bed, her juice still coating his skin. *Those abs, fuck, they're chiseled.* She ran her tongue along the crease, over the tight skin, sucking back the taste of her arousal that still coated his skin before taking Adam's thick cock into her mouth.

Trent speared her from behind — hard, fast and with no time to adjust. He was in her and pounding her so that her head was moving along Adam's shaft, taking him back into her throat. Adam reached forward to play with her tits, rolling her nipples between his fingers and thumbs, twisting and flicking, rubbing, pinching, soothing. He played with both, making them ache and throb, heating with the attention and sending jolts of pure pleasure right down to her pussy. She spasmed, holding Trent's cock tightly inside her as he thrust over and over again. He stuck his thumb into her asshole, wedging deep and pushing down hard so that he was practically rubbing his own cock inside her pussy.

She moaned around Adam's dick, her body rocking, humming with another orgasm on the rise.

"We could both be in her at the same time." Trent panted, stilling his movements.

Sabine looked up at Adam, catching his eyes. *Did I just hear that right?*

Adam nodded, a slow smile creeping onto his face. "Stuff her full of cock."

Trent slapped her ass hard, with an open palm. She yelped at the sting, so he did it again and again, until she was moving away from him, trying to avoid the next slap. He pulled his dick out, wrapped his arms around her and flipped her onto him. Chest to chest, him staring up into her eyes.

"I love you, Sabine."

She smiled, kissed him hard, then pushed herself up. "I love you too, Trent." Then she glided her pussy over his dick and rode him until they were both slick with sweat.

"Ready?" Adam climbed onto the bed, his weight moving them slightly backward.

Sabine looked at Trent, one last unspoken question there.

Trent nodded. "Hell yes! Hurry up and stick your dick in her, man!"

Sabine felt the surreal rush of the impossibly of this. That Trent would go for it? It almost brought tears to her eyes.

She smiled instead, though, then lifted her ass in the air, not enough to dislodge Trent's cock but enough that Adam could slip his in.

He moved closer to her and she felt the cool sensation of lube sliding over her asshole. He gripped her hips, nudging her with his dick then easing slowly, so very slowly, inside her.

Two giant cocks filled her and the sensation was more amazing than she could have imagined. They were better than dildos, pulsing with energy, jolting her from the inside. Once Adam was in as far as he could go, Sabine's ass stretching out for him, Trent started to move, slowly gliding his cock out, then in.

"I can feel your dick," Trent breathed.

"I can feel yours, man." Adam grunted.

Sabine, sandwiched between the two, was in ecstasy. She closed her eyes and let the overwhelming sensations take control.

She didn't know who was playing with her breasts, whose fingers were teasing her nipples. All she knew was that it felt so damn good, so damn incredible to move her body with these men. Her tight asshole barely accommodated Adam. His movements continued in a slow and steady glide, pulling out of her as Trent slammed deep within. And that was how it went. The men figured out a rhythm, one gliding back while the other slammed her hard — then the other pulled out so that another dick could pump deep inside her.

Every part of her relaxed and she let the men have her, let them fuck her, let them love her and worship her body. And she did feel worshipped, like a goddess.

She spasmed hard, her orgasm taking her by surprise, a wallop of sensation that she first felt in her stomach, like a hard flutter, before it raced along her spine. It rushed over her body, every nerve ending sparking at the same time. She cried out, opening her eyes as her climax roared through her.

And there was Trent, staring at her with such love, such desire, that she did tear up, overwhelmed by the emotion of it all.

Her orgasm lasted forever, it seemed, carrying her through as Adam pumped jets of cum into her ass, his whole body spasming. Trent bellowed his own release, pumping her pussy full as well.

They collapsed in unison, Sabine falling to the side, in between the men, with Adam's dick only barely encased in her ass and Trent slipping out of her pussy.

They were sweat-covered and gasping for breath.

"I've never done that before," Sabine admitted.

"No way!" Trent laughed. "We just popped your double penetration cherry?"

Sabine's face was already flushed, so he probably wouldn't see the blush there. "I've always wanted to, but I'd never found the right guys to do the job."

Trent pushed himself up. "You hear that, Adam? We were her firsts!"

Adam chuckled when Trent offered him a high five. They did their manly congratulations then Adam slipped out of the bed. "I'm going to clean up and get back to work."

Sabine looked over her shoulder at him, grateful as Trent slipped the sheets over her shivering body. "Thanks, Adam." Fresh tears bubbled. She didn't brush them away.

"Always a pleasure, Mistress," he said. Then he turned, grabbed his clothes and went into the shower.

"You really haven't ever done that before?" Trent pulled her attention back to him.

She nuzzled into his chest. "Nope."

"You were saving yourself?"

"I guess, yeah. It had to be the right guys, ya know?"

Trent lifted her chin. "The right guys and the right girl," he corrected, then he kissed her, softly, passionately, letting her know just how much he truly loved her.

Epilogue

Cowan Enterprises had a top-notch team. Adam was head of security, as always, Sabine ruled all things and now, Trent was the new public relations officer, leading a killer creative team that he'd assembled.

They were working on a new campaign to launch a line of fetish gear that Trent had taken a particular liking to. There were lots of items to play with pleasure and pain, soft and hard, smooth and rough—and durable too. It was great stuff.

"Maybe if you're a good girl, I'll use this on you later," Trent teased as he smacked a feathered paddle over his palm.

Sabine giggled. "A good girl or a bad girl?" She winked as she glanced up from her computer screen.

They sat in her office, across from one another at the large meeting table. They'd fucked on it first thing that morning—a little wake-me-up to get the day going. Trent liked it when she wore a summer dress. It was easy to flip her skirt up and stick his dick in whichever hole she wanted.

"Mm-m, good point." He put the paddle back into its case. There was no time for fun and games at the moment, though, not with the creative team on the way. They had four hours set aside for brainstorming new ideas and Trent was full of them. Working for Sabine was way more fun than Morgan and Miller had ever been.

And he had no regrets — well, except for maybe one.

"I heard that Ellie's looking at ten years, at least," Trent said, his voice edged with sadness. He'd read a news article while he was waiting for Sabine to shower, the headline catching him off guard. Adam and Sabine had been handling things with regards to the investigation. Trent barely had to interact with the detectives at all.

Somehow — through Sabine's contacts, no doubt — they had also gotten more dirt on Roy, and the investigation against him was all over the media. Even so, seeing Ellie's name as a headline had been a surprise to Trent.

"She has the opportunity to make a deal." Sabine looked up from her computer. "The choice is hers."

That had been his one stipulation, to give Ellie an out, an opportunity to lessen her punishment. The ball was in her court.

"I know," he sighed. That didn't make it any easier to swallow.

"Hey, messenger boy," Sabine teased — a throwback nickname to their first night together all those months ago. "We've got ten minutes. Why don't you see how many whacks you can get in before the team arrives? If you can make it hard to sit, I'll give you a blow job at the restaurant later."

Trent's eyes widened, his smile stretched his face and hurt his cheeks. "You got it, Mistress."

He picked up the paddle and stood. "Lift that skirt and let me see that pretty plump little ass."

She moved around her desk slowly, rolling her hips in that tantalizing way she had. She trailed her fingers along the buttons of her dress, like she was just about to take it off.

"Nah-uh. I want that dress to stay on. It's hot as fuck."

She ran her hand over her breasts. "Oh, yeah? Do you like this one the best?" She moved around so that her back was facing Trent then flipped her skirt up to reveal her juicy ass.

He smacked the paddle against his hand, his cock jolting at the sight of her beautiful skin. She arched her back so he could see her glistening pussy, then she looked over her shoulder at him with a coy little smile. "I think I've been a very bad girl."

Trent nodded, moving without really thinking about it, his mind on sinking his throbbing cock deep into her cunt. He grabbed her ass, kneading roughly. "You have been a bad girl, Sabine. Filthy too."

He lifted his hand at the same time he brought the paddle down with a *whack*.

Sabine cried out, shifting her head forward and bracing her arms on the desk so she could take his next smack. He reached around to cup her breast and wedged his pant-covered dick against her ass, rubbing so she'd know just how hot he was for her.

She moaned, bucking against him.

"Do you want my dick, baby?" He pinched her nipple through the fabric of her dress.

"Yes, you know I do."

He pulled back. "Yes, *Sir*." Then he brought the paddle down once again.

"Yes, Sir!" she yelped.

Her ass cheeks were a nice rosy red by the time he'd finished with her. His cock was throbbing so fucking hard that he thought he'd die, and he couldn't help himself when he tossed the paddle aside then spun her around. He ripped her dress right down the middle so he could suck on her tits while at the same time pushing her back until her ass hit the edge of her desk. He sheathed himself to the hilt, fucking her brains out as he pinched and licked at her delicious nipples.

She wrapped her legs around his hips, taking the pounding with sexy-sounding moans, knocking all kinds of shit off her desk to crash on the floor while he pounded the fuck out of her pussy.

When her orgasm rose, her moans turned wild. He gripped her hips and stared into her eyes, drilling her with everything he had, including all the love in his heart.

Sabine was his and he was hers. This? This was the good life.

Want to see more like this?
Here's a taster for you to enjoy!

Luca's Lessons
Deana Birch & Amelia Foster

Excerpt

A silver foil wrapper tumbled down the stone walkway along the Limmat River, and Luca stepped to the side, his arms crossed. A giggling young couple with too many piercings for his personal preference hurried by, unaware of the menacing, forgotten paper. In his dark suit, crisp white shirt and matching silk navy tie, he waited.

The improperly disposed-of litter flopped one more time, trapped itself at the edge of the stone wall and, away from the light breeze, rested. Satisfied by his small conquest — surely it was his will that had brought its journey to an end — Luca smirked. He walked over, picked it up and secured its fate in a wire bin. A pestering thought of germs poked at his side, but he brushed his hands together at a job well done and continued on his path to the private bank.

While the inconvenience had been a distraction, it had been welcomed. Early and eager were two qualities he admired, but not in himself. He reached for the door of the gray, historic building at exactly seven minutes past his scheduled appointment. *Perfetto.*

After a brief check through security, including a confirmation of his identity, he climbed the two flights of stairs to the private bank of Steinmetz and Favre.

The heavy wooden doors of the suite opened to sleek metal-and-cream marble that created a stark contrast to the building's dated exterior. But the interior did not surprise Luca. He'd already seen the clean, powerful reception in the magazine article about the youngest woman entrepreneur in the history of private banking.

And it was no mistake he'd sought out Claire Favre. Young, driven and on-the-rise was exactly the kind of mind he wanted handling his soon-to-be-acquired secret business. The piece about her and her partner in the weekly publication inserted into the Sunday paper had done more than pique his interest. Fortunately, Luca's reputation and family history had provided enough of a motivation that he'd obtained an appointment without too much delay.

He gave his name to the young, just-above-cheap-suited man behind the massive desk and took a seat in the black leather club chair. Magazines in four different languages were fanned on the iron table next to him. He aligned the one on top to sync with the others and the rhythmed echo of high heels ricocheting off the hallowed walls made him look up.

Madonna mia.

The picture had done her no justice. Claire Favre's sharp hip bones pointed behind the fabric of her tight black skirt and they swayed in a hypnotizing motion as she drew nearer. The formfitting blazer matched the skirt, and a pink silk blouse formed a deep V below. Different from the photo, where her blonde locks had been loose and casual as she'd smiled, her hair was now pulled back into a low, tight bun and her lips remained firmly locked together.

Luca stood, happy his height put him at an advantage, and buttoned his jacket at the waist. The momentary shock of her in-person beauty sank into his gut. It had no business in his throat or chest.

"Herr Bernardi." She extended her small, manicured hand but barely smiled.

"English, please." Luca ignored the slight jump in his heart rate as they touched.

"As you wish." Her light shrug remained formal.

Surely a coincidence.

He narrowed his eyes.

Ms. Favre's smile grew tighter and she spun around. "My office is just down the hall."

Luca followed the banker and stared at the back of her exposed neck. He would not check out her ass, not in a professional setting where the woman deserved respect. He would not.

He did. He most certainly did. And damn it all to hell and back if his palm didn't twitch with desire.

When the penance of being a gentleman and walking behind a woman to whom he owed respect—not ogling—had finished, he squared his shoulders at the threshold of her office and renewed his purpose—business.

Ms. Favre ushered him to a cubed leather chair opposite her desk and he reached for the button of his jacket while she floated to the other side of the impressive oak plank.

A quick glance of her surroundings revealed nothing—no framed photos of her and the late husband the article had referred to or children it had not hinted at. Truly nothing. This woman was clean, uncomplicated and professional—everything Luca desired in a banker…and perhaps other things.

"Please," she said and motioned to the seat behind him. With a quick brush on the back of her skirt—*is hand jealousy a thing?*—she gracefully sat. "Tell me what brings you here, Mr. Bernardi."

Where to begin? The long and challenging path of fully respecting and refining one's own needs? The obvious motivation of a man-made success? Best to start with the not-so-shocking. One never knows.

In the warmest, most casual tone he could muster he said, "I am in negotiations to buy a business. A private club, actually. And I was hoping to keep said investment separate from my others."

Her blue-gray gaze pierced him and she drew her light, thin eyebrows together. "You have a business you'd like to hide, and you want to use my bank to do so?"

"No." Convincing her was going to take some massaging, especially since the bulk of his wealth would not be coming along for the ride. "I have a business I'd like to keep to myself, but I'd like you to handle investing and growing the worth of the account."

Claire crossed her fingers on the desk and circled a thumb slowly into the opposite palm.

"Is it an illegal business?" she asked.

"No, but it is private, much like your bank." Luca flattened his lips and fought a smile. The woman calmed herself with touch. He admired and recognized the gesture. In a cold room full of stark decorations, her softness slammed into him.

He blinked. Business. And the need to hide his new project.

"And what is this soon-to-be-acquired opportunity?" She creased her pink lips.

There was the catch. The hitch. The hard-sell.

He stared into her eyes. "A private club."

She stilled her hands and cocked an eyebrow. "A misogynistic group of racist old men smoking cigars and plotting world domination?"

Interesting choice of words.

"No." This time he allowed the smile to shine. Her spunk and terseness must have helped her along the way.

But what way? According to the magazine article, she was barely thirty years old, and her private schooling, with winters in Gstaad and springs outside of Geneva, had assured her enough wealthy contacts for life. Her path and its perks had been easy — a silver spoon and a glass slipper.

"Are women welcome in your club, Mr. Bernardi?"

Her chest rose then fell slowly.

"Very much so." He dipped his chin.

She'd mentioned it twice now. Maybe empowering women was her motive.

Luca continued, "I welcome all to my club, Ms. Favre. The members and I pride ourselves on acceptance."

This brought a slight tilt to her head and what Luca hoped was a glimmer in her hazy eyes.

"All? That doesn't sound too private."

Her objection was welcomed with fervor, the familiar heat Luca longed for in a challenge. That, and her 'As you wish' comment from reception, braided into a perfect rope of feisty and submissive — not that the powerful woman before him would ever admit to wanting to surrender herself to the will of another.

But, contrary to what were probably her beliefs, she had all the signs. Her manners were impeccable. Her attention to detail…perfection. And that softness… The gentle side of her that Luca would bet his portfolio she didn't think people saw — but he did. He knew exactly the kind of woman who sat in front of him.

"I assure you that the membership fee secures the privacy," he said with a quick nod.

"And what is the membership fee? If I may ask?"

You may. Such lovely manners.

"Fifty thousand euros initially, plus another fifty thousand a year. On top of that, there are certain benefits that members may or may not choose to acquire. But, essentially, ten million would be my earnings in the first year."

She smiled curtly. The minimum balance to open most private banks in Switzerland was usually around a million francs. With a promise of more, maybe the risk of taking on what appeared to be a seedy client would dissolve.

"What exactly transpires at your club, Mr. Bernardi?" Her business etiquette remained flawless.

Well, that would depend entirely on which room one would peep into. But there was no reason to beat around the bush.

"Exploration of one's boundaries, Ms. Favre." Luca met her stare with heavy eyes.

"Sex. You plan to run a high society sex club." Her tone was flat, almost bored.

How could she hold his gaze? He was certain she was more a bottom than a top.

"I'm interested in continuing the initial goal of the founder, who provides a safe environment for all genders to escape without worries or hassles. It has been a tradition for years that every member sign a confidentiality agreement. It covers everything done and witnessed behind the closed, or sometimes open" — he tilted his head — "doors of the club."

Claire Favre appeared to remain unfazed. *Is she?*

She looked past Luca and he studied the pale, sweet skin exposed from her neck to her chest. From the lack of freckles and spots, it hadn't seen much sun over the summer. He knew its shade well, the perfect cream that would flush pink with proper stimulation.

Luca lifted his gaze. He would not be caught dreaming about bunching up her skirt and examining the most sensitive areas of her body. *Business*, he reminded himself.

"Might I ask why you thought *I* would be the right banker for your secret investment?"

Luca was still very much denying the answer himself. The woman had intrigued more than his financial affairs when he'd seen her in the photo.

"Empowerment, Ms. Favre. We're in the same business. You want to empower —"

She raised a hand and scoffed. He'd finally rattled her.

"I fail to see how tying up women and spanking them with riding crops is empowering." Her expression must have been attempting to scold him.

Hilarious.

Ah, the misconceptions. The fantasized, glorified, utter wrongness in the perception of the lifestyle... Luca had hoped a woman of Claire's status would have been better read than what popular opinion had painted as the BDSM culture. But alas, stereotypes were indeed festering wounds.

Luca curled his index finger around his mouth and tucked the opposite hand under his elbow.

She sat behind her desk, eyes slightly narrowed and waiting, oh so patiently with her hint of challenge, for his response. The blend was intoxicating.

Before the stirrings of his under-thoughts could bubble to the surface, he said, "I'd like to prove you wrong. The best way to do that I think would be to show you."

Her eyelids fluttered and the rosy flush he'd been trying to deny he craved crept up her neck. Claire swallowed hard.

Sorry, Ms. Favre. Flexing my mental muscle is an unbreakable yet delicious habit.

"Excuse me?" she managed.

Luca cleared his throat. "There are, perhaps, images you have about what goes on in a private setting such as my future club—images that, while they may scratch at the surface of truth, do only that…scratch."

Her skin returned to its cream natural state and Luca grieved the departure of the pink.

He continued, "Why don't you visit? Take a tour. I'm sure you'll find that it's just as much a legitimate business as the pesticides that kill millions of bees every year. Hopefully, more. I assure you that no one gets hurt unless they want to." Another man might have winked, but Luca only shifted his jaw instead.

She stiffened her posture. "You want me to come to a club and watch people get spanked and have sex?"

He grinned. "You seem rather fixated on the spanking part."

She rolled her eyes.

That would never do.

"I'm not fixated on anything. I'm just wondering… If your business is so much on the up and up, why would you want to hide it in my bank, because it doesn't seem like any of your other sources of income are shifting into my vaults with it? And secondly, why then, would I take a risk on you, a stranger to me, for a venture that you would like to brush under the rug?"

Luca crossed his foot over the opposite knee and adjusted in his chair.

"To answer your questions…" He twisted the platinum watch below his starched cuff. "For starters, perhaps I am interested in having some privacy on this matter and wish to not mix it with the accounts that have been in my family for decades. I am well aware of the labels that accompany my lifestyle. I still have a sweet, aging grandmother, and I have no intention of killing her with rumors of my sex life."

Claire's hands folded once again, but this time she rolled her shoulders back and shivered.

"And secondly, I read about you. I know you are a perfect balance of risk-taker and security. Much like anyone, I'd like to see my money grow. As I have no friends who are clients of yours, I feel the risk is mutual."

She sat back and tapped her delicate thumbs together three times.

Stalemate.

Her gaze ran the length of Luca and when it met his, she gave a slight purse of her mouth. "When?"

He wet his lips.

"Friday or Saturday night. You'll need to sign a non-disclosure agreement and you won't be able to visit the higher floors. But you will get a sense that the members are as normal as you and me." He paused at the brief fantasy of her in his private suite. "And you will see the respect and consent of a tight community."

Her eyes raked over him again. *A good sign?* He couldn't tell.

"I'll think about it."

She rose, as did he, and he followed her to the door.

"I'll see myself out." Luca nodded. There was no way he could follow that ass down the hall after he'd discovered how her skin could blush with just a few words.

"As you wish," she said.

Despite the brakes halting in his mind, Luca exited her office.

How had she known? How could she have possibly known the symphony of music those words were to his ears?

Home of Erotic Romance

Sign up for our newsletter and find out about all our romance book releases, eBook sales and promotions, sneak peeks and FREE romance books!

About the Author

Angela Addams is an author of many naughty things. She believes that the written word is an amazing tool for crafting the most erotic of scenarios and likes telling stories about normal people getting down and dirty and falling in love. Enthralled by the paranormal at an early age, Angela also spends a lot of her time thinking up new story ideas that involve supernatural creatures in everyday situations.

She is an avid tattoo collector, a total book hoarder, and loves anything covered in chocolate...except for bugs.

She lives in Ontario, Canada in an old, creaky house, with her husband, children and four moody cats.

Angela loves to hear from readers. You can find her contact information, website details and author profile page at https://www.totallybound.com

www.ingramcontent.com/pod-product-compliance
Lightning Source LLC
Chambersburg PA
CBHW020418180626
46812CB00003B/1038